Down to Paradise

by
Bill Rhode

DORRANCE PUBLISHING CO., INC.
PITTSBURGH, PENNSYLVANIA 15222

ISBN # 0-8059-4251-3
Printed in the United States of America

First Printing

For information or to order additional books, please write:
Dorrance Publishing Co., Inc.
643 Smithfield Street
Pittsburgh, Pennsylvania 15222
U.S.A.

CHAPTER | ONE

The alarm clock within the bedroom, went off at 6:30 A.M. Martha Maloney stirred beside her husband. It was time to get the kids up for school. It was usually her role to rouse the children and serve their breakfast. If only they could afford a hired lady as did her sister, Jane, then she could sleep a bit later in the day.

She slid out from under the covers to a sitting position on the left side of the bed. She sat there for a brief moment. *Why in the hell do I have to be the one to get these kids up while my husband, John, always grabs that extra ten minutes rest before rolling out of bed. It just isn't fair,* she thought. *And this tiny bedroom of this damn tiny house is so cramped.*

She arose, stretching her lithesome body, trying to shake the kinks out of it. She reached for her housecoat, donning it and tying the belt about her waist. This life married to a pilot was just not all it was supposed to be. Not enough money for this, not enough money for that. Too small a house, you couldn't afford this, you couldn't afford that. She envied her sister, Jane, who seemingly had everything.

Martha strode into the girl's bedroom, waking up both Kelly, aged nine years, and Patricia, aged seven years. If the Maloney's had anything more than Jane had, it was the kids. Jane only had one child.

Martha made her way to the kitchen where she started putting on the coffee pot, setting the table for the jumbo box of Crunchy–Munchies and canned fruit while John stirred up out of bed and sat on the edge of it trying to gather his thoughts together. He was scheduled to fly at 9:00 A.M. He was trying to remember what day it was, Wednesday or Thursday.

He had to wait for his kids to wash in the bathroom. He reached for his bathrobe, wrapping it about him. "Maybe Martha is right. This house is just too small. Only one bathroom for the four of us," he said aloud. Hell, what could he do about it? He was only pulling down about $600 a week for all the flying he was doing.

He was just getting sick and tired of all the carping at him. Could he help it if baby sister Jane's lawyer husband made $200,000 a year and had the best of everything while he, John, made only $31,200 a year?

He made his way to the bathroom and turned on the water spigots in the bathtub. Ten minutes later, he was drying himself off and reaching for his toothbrush and razor.

John made his way from the bathroom back to the bedroom, where he finished dressing. In the nearby kitchen he could hear Martha yelling at the kids to hurry up and brush their teeth and finish dressing. The school bus would be by at 7:45 A.M., and time was pressing. Then Kelly asked for some change.

"Mom, can we each have a dollar for a milkshake at lunchtime? All the kids have them."

"I don't have any extra dollars right now," Martha allowed. "If your father could make a decent living instead of all that pleasure flying, maybe we would have some extra funds around here."

John was getting sick of all those snide remarks here and there. They were not doing too bad, he thought. All the bills are currently paid. This Cape Cod house was their own, and the car was nearly paid for. Once in a while they could enjoy dinner out together, but lately Martha had it in for him.

He made his way into the kitchen and sat down at the table.

"Hi, Dad!" yelled the kids in unison.

"Good morning, girls."

Martha glared at him. He reached toward the toaster and extracted two slices of toast and began buttering them in preparation for the two poached eggs she was preparing in a pan of boiling water.

Presently the girls donned their sweaters and grabbed their books and lunch baskets, kissing John and Martha goodbye. After their departure, Martha started on him again.

"Do you suppose I might get twenty dollars from you to buy the kids some needed items?" she asked sarcastically.

"You know I just have expense money on me," he replied.

"You always seem to have some money on you," she replied belligerently.

"I have eleven dollars on me. The car needs gas, and I need lunch money for the next four days. What do you think I'm doing, keeping another woman?"

"I'm damn sick of this pauper's life I lead with you," she shouted at him. "Jane's husband gives her everything she wants. A big beautiful home, her own car, servants, everything. What have I had from you?"

"I, too, am sick of this life with you!" he bellowed back at her. "You are never satisfied. I am trying to give you everything. What more can I do? You have your own home, even if it is mortgaged. You have two kids to her one. I don't make anywhere near the money he does, but what can I do about it? I'm trying."

"You call this a home?" she screamed at him. "I call it a dump. The whole damn place needs redecorating. Why don't you give up sitting on your ass in an airplane with girl students and go out and get a big job in industry. Then maybe, just maybe, we could have something around here besides old, decrepit, shabby furniture."

"What the hell is old about the furniture all of a sudden? We just replaced it two years ago. What is bugging you now?" he shot back at her. She made her way to the bathroom and slammed the door shut. He downed his coffee and got up from the table. It seemed as though this was the sum total of their married life lately. Constant wrangling over what they didn't have and what she thought they should have.

He donned his leather flight jacket and paused outside the bathroom door hoping he might embrace her for a minute before he left. The days at the airport were getting longer with the advent of spring, and by the time he got back home at night and had his supper, the nights whizzed by so fast.

"I'm going now, Babe. Open up, will you?" She did not answer him. "I'm leaving now, Honey. Open the door, will you please?" Still no answer. He shrugged his shoulders and made his way out to his three–year–old sedan. He waved to his neighbor and got into his car.

What could be bugging Martha lately? He was a flyer before she came into his life. Eleven years before, he was a charter and flight instructor. He married Martha and then he was inducted with the Air National Guard for duty in the Persian Gulf War. They had two children. When he returned to civilian life, he resumed flying as before. It seems they were very happy in those days.

He had put $2,000 down on this Cape Cod in a development, and they were very compatible back then. These Cape Cod houses were four–room bungalows, stylish in appearance but were diminutive, with two bed-rooms, a parlor and a kitchen. The attics could be enlarged with dormers to increase occupancy. They were, for the most part, reasonably priced.

All these houses were similar in appearance except for their variety in paint colors—red, blue, green, white, pink, or orange depending on one's preference. Some referred to this type of house as a "starter" home. A deposit to moving up to a higher–priced house in the future. It was their own home.

Their two healthy daughters were a prime example of their earlier devotion to each other. Then he gave up the air–taxi part of his flying as it necessitated his flying in all kinds of weather. He then took this position with the Zenith Flying Service as a flight instructor and sometimes charter pilot at the Sky Harbor Airport in New Jersey.

As his two children were growing up, he had tried to get an airline pilot's position. But he was just too old, they told him. Imagine, too old at thirty–one years. They wanted youngsters twenty–two to twenty-nine years so as to get a longer return out of the expensive training that was provided by the airlines.

Even at that, he had managed to make a comfortable livelihood. Everything had worked out fine for them as a family until....

Martha's younger sister, Jane, had gotten married two years previously to a lawyer. Jane and her husband, Roger, had taken possession of this large, palatial, eleven–room house with large picture windows and patios. They now had three high–priced cars, one child, servants, and every comfort it seemed.

The damn cost of living kept on rising, and there were constant increases in taxes, medical insurance, routine expenses and food–stuff. The General Aviation Industry at private airports and flying schools, never seemed to keep pace with the cost of living in other endeavors. He loved to fly. It was his lifetime career.

Yet, as a flight instructor and charter pilot, he never seemed to make an overabundant livelihood. The glamour of the job was there but unfortunately, not enough money in this comparatively new budding industry.

A half hour later, he pulled onto the parking lot of the Sky Harbor Airport, shut off his car ignition, and headed for the Zenith Flying Service Flight Office.

CHAPTER | TWO

As John walked into the flight office, he was greeted with a series of "Good morning, John, you old buzzard" type of expressions; others with a "Hello, John, you old kiteflyer;" and other greetings such as "Hello John, you balloon–strafed kiwi." He laughed. This was but another reason why he liked it here at the airport. Every morning, no matter how blue you might feel, the airport gang dug their needles into you with their light comedy and quips.

He walked over to the flight dispatcher's desk and scanned the appointment sheet. He was booked to fly at 9:00 A.M. and 11:00 A.M. with a charter flight to Pittsburgh at 1:00 P.M. Ruth Reynolds, the dispatcher, briefed him on the weather.

"Clear all day; high, broken, and scattered clouds. Wind at 15 M.P.H. Beautiful."

Ruth always gave him a big smile when he walked in. He appeared to be more of a man than the silly younger crowd, she thought. Sure, he was married and had two children but he sure had sex appeal, she reasoned. She also answered the UNICOM, the radio communication system to other aircraft from this office.

A few moments later, John's student strode in and the two of them made their way out to the early morning flight line. The student pre–flighted the aircraft as John had often times showed him how, and after checking the fuel load and oil level in the engine, both men climbed into the two–seater Century training plane.

They started up the engine, whirling the propeller about, and taxied slowly to the end of Runway 22. After checking out the engine and its dual ignition systems, controls, and instruments, they turned out onto the runway. The student fed full throttle to it, and they sped down the runway and into the sky. They climbed out around the rectangular flight pattern.

Shortly after a series of landings, they were coming in for the final touchdown. The trainer was gliding in about one minute behind another plane that had just landed. Over the treetops they glided. Then as they leveled off and settled to the runway, the student seemed to get lost as he landed, misjudging the distance to the runway, letting the plane get away from him.

The student turned the plane off the runway to the parallel taxi strip. He was capable of the takeoffs but not too sharp on the landings. Another hour or two of dual instruction would be necessary before letting him solo.

They taxied back to a position on the flight line, just in front of the flight office. Both re–entered the office, where John gave him a few more encouraging oral lessons, signed his pilot log book and made an additional appointment for the following week. Then, shortly after the student departed.

"Ruth, I'm going over to the snack bar for coffee," John notified the dispatcher. "Want me to bring you some back?"

"No, thank you," she replied. "I'll meet you over there in a few minutes, if you are buying."

"Okay, I'll buy. How long will you be?" he asked.

"Just as soon as I get these two students up on their solo flights and Marian relieves me," she answered.

He made his way over to the airport snack bar and pushed his way through the doorway. The airport snack bar was quite the place for a theme setting. It reeked of the atmosphere and color of flying with pictures on the walls and an old wooden propeller hanging over the doorway. The proprietor, Herman Meyer, was an old Luftwaffe pilot from World War Two. After the war was over, he emigrated to the United States and now was running this snack bar just to be near flyers and flying.

John took a position on a stool at the counter and ordered two cups of coffee while securing the stool next to him for Ruth. He liked Ruth. She seemed like a nice kid. But as far as anything else, that was it. When it came to his love life, Martha was his one and only. If only Martha could be made to realize that.

Ruth soon hurried in and sat down next to John for a fast cup of coffee.

"How are you making out with Tom, Ruth?" he asked only to make trivial conversation.

"I quit him last night," she answered. "I found out he was two–timing me. He has another steady girl besides me. The dirty stinker."

John laughed. "How does a guy afford two girls? I can't even afford one."

"Its so hard to find a decent guy these days," Ruth continued. "Every guy you meet is out for sex and nothing more."

"Ruth, if I wasn't married, I'd go chasing after you myself," he grinned.

She smiled her big golden smile at him and then bluntly replied: "If you weren't married, I'd let you chase after me until I caught you."

The coffee finished, both of them returned to the flight office. Ruth was a very attractive brunette of twenty years. She was not too sophisticated as yet, while trying to hold onto certain of her morals in a changing world of values. It was just that her ideal of a man had not as yet crossed her horizon. She secretly liked John a lot. He was tall, well proportioned, and poised, and always polite and considerate. He had been in warfare and seen something of the world. Yet she knew John was not to be had and she accepted that.

At 11:00 A.M., John took off for an hour of instrument instruction with a student who was trying to complete his private pilot's course. His wife, Martha, had made the remark about him always flying with women, whereas only about one out of six students were females.

It was noontime now, and John and his student landed on Runway 22 and taxied back to the flight line where they parked the highwing training plane. He signed off the student's log book and made an additional appointment with him. Then he hurried to the snack bar.

He took his place at the crowded counter and ordered just coffee and a doughnut. He had put five dollars worth of fuel into his car and after coffee with Ruth, he was now down to two dollars. He passed the lunch hour at the counter with another of the many private plane owners on the field, unaware that Ruth was watching him from a booth.

In the designated choice of a runway direction for the day, it had to do with the wind direction. The runway in use was numbered by the compass direction of the headwind. A wind from the west meant a compass heading of 270 degrees or Runway 27. A wind from the east meant a compass direction of 90 degrees or Runway 9. South was Runway 18, north Runway 36.

At 1:00 P.M., he took off with two passengers and their baggage for the trip to Pittsburgh. He always liked these charter trips. There was no struggling with students. You just took off and flew yourself. The trip to Pittsburgh was three hundred miles west which, with the big four seater Skyline aircraft with its 220 horsepower engine, would mean two hours of flying time each way.

The vast countryside unraveled below him—farmland, woods, mountains, towns, and cities. This was the beauty of flight that had always enticed him. Flying was like a woman; the lure was always there. At 3:00 P.M. he landed at the Allegheny County Airport, discharging his two passengers and their baggage. He topped off his fuel tanks, and after a quick cola drink, he was heading back to Sky Harbor in New Jersey. He used his Zenith Flying Service credit card to pay for the fuel.

Unknown to John, Ruth Reynolds was developing a big crush on him. She knew he wouldn't be back in time when she was ready to leave the airport at her normal quitting time at 5:00 P.M., yet she just had to find a way to be with him or near him more often.

For several months now she had her eyes on John. She did not want an affair with a married man but if she could just be near the guy and enjoy his proximity, she would be content. She made up her mind now to take flying lessons with him on the weekend when she was off.

When John returned to Sky Harbor from Pittsburgh, he was scheduled to fly again at 6:00 P.M. with another student. After terminating his flying slightly past 7:00 P.M., he pointed his car toward home on Melody Lane. It was a half hour drive each way to and from the airport. In these late spring days, he never got around to eating his main big meal until 8:00 P.M. Then he spent a few minutes with his kids and glanced at a newspaper.

When he walked in, Martha greeted him with stony silence.

"Hello, Babe," he said and reached for her. She dodged him.

He sat down to supper with young Patty on his lap. At least his kids did not hate him. Shortly after both little ones went off to bed. He then sought a conversation with Martha but she would not oblige him.

At 10:00 P.M., she made plans to retire early without notifying him. She just quietly left the parlor and, within a few seconds, he heard the squeak of the bed as she climbed in for the night.

He folded the newspaper and laid it on the side table, getting up to douse the lamplight. When he climbed into the bed next to Martha, she would not acknowledge his presence. He reached out his arm for her, trying to drag her around to face him. She froze like the Polar Icecap.

"Martha, what is happening to us? Why are you acting this way? I love you. Please turn around and talk for a few minutes," he begged.

She remained mute. He grabbed her about the waist and vainly tried to bring her around. She flew at him like a tigress.

"Take your damn hands off of me. Leave me alone." He very quietly turned around and went to sleep. *There was always tomorrow,* he thought.

CHAPTER | THREE

It was Friday morning. The alarm clock went off, and Martha once again got up out of bed to get her youngsters ready for school. Shortly thereafter John dragged his big, muscular body out of bed and headed for the bathtub. When he walked into the kitchen, Martha scowled at him. He hadn't really expected her to do otherwise on this dreary morning. Over the breakfast table she finally broke her stony silence.

"Jane invited us over there for supper tonight. Do you think you can bring yourself to taking us over there?" she asked.

He thought for a few minutes and then replied in kind. "I'll go over there on one condition. That you smile and treat me civilly."

She did not answer him but bent over the sink to start washing the dishes. He looked toward her. She had not had relations with him in two weeks. He got up and reached gently for her. He forced her into his arms trying to break the cake of ice she had built about herself.

"Babe, what is wrong?"

"I'll tell you after tonight," she replied. "Now let go of me. You are hurting me."

John finished flying that evening and headed home toward Melody Lane. He would have a late supper tonight and had no lunch during the day as his pocket money was down. When he pulled onto the gravel driveway, his kids greeted him from the doorway. "Daddy's home," they bellowed in unison.

He strode into the house and removed his flying clothes and entered the bathroom to bathe and shave. Then he donned a clean white shirt and tie and took down one of two suits out of the bedroom closet. Now fully dressed, he gathered his brood about him and headed for his car. Martha still gave him a cold shoulder for an entree.

He pointed his car toward Jane and Roger's house on Wishbone Lane in Putney Township. What a large, beautiful dollhouse they resided in. It was set back on two acres of fine landscape, built of grey fieldstone and almost every window seemed a large store window with vertical blinds and fancy curtains. Every room was ablaze with lights. As they parked on the frontal driveway, Martha's mouth watered.

Every time Martha saw this seeming palace, she went into a trance. "Why should baby sister Jane have everything in just two years of married life while John and I struggle just to live very frugally?"

A young maid dressed in a very becoming black uniform greeted them at the entrance. Just behind the maid was Jane herself, welcoming them inside the impressive entrance.

The inside of the house was fabulous. The rooms were so expansive. There was high–priced furniture all about. John took it all in stride. Sure, it was all nice, every bit of it, but why drool? If you couldn't afford this magnanimous pattern of living, why get hung up about it? Roger then came down out of the master bedroom above them and shook hands with John. Then they all entered the playroom where cocktails were served with little snacks on which the kids would chew on.

The cook came into the playroom and announced that dinner was ready. One by one they all marched single file into the well–furnished dining room with its large crystal chandelier and potted ferns.

"We don't even have a dining room," Martha loudly proclaimed. "We eat in the kitchen in our joint." John winced once again. This was no doubt what was presumably bugging Martha, these fancy trappings.

The cook came out of the kitchen and set salad bowls in front of them, followed shortly by hot bowls of soup. Then the main course of steak and vegetables arrived, followed by special ice cream molds, then finished with coffee and *creme de menthe*. After leaving the long table, Jane showed them a couple of large, rare paintings she had procured for the parlor and also some pieces she had been given by Roger, from a prominent New York jeweler.

Finally at 11:00 P.M., John had a bellyful. He graciously announced that he had to get up and fly the next day for a busy weekend of flying. They then left Jane's house in his cruddy–looking sedan.

"If it is cruddy looking, it was just honest dust from the airport," John allowed. "Also, if its windows were dirty, it was from the kid's hands rubbing the windows. That was all."

He pulled up into the driveway of his house on Melody Lane, and they all retired for the night. Martha would not speak a word to him. As far as she was concerned, he could go to hell from now on. He helped her put the kids to bed with a kiss on the cheek and a clasp of covers up to their necks. They both retired a short distance to their own bedroom. Once again he reached for her and she put him off.

"Martha, I need you. Please, let me love you."

"I want nothing to do with you until you decide to support your family in a decent way. Then and only then shall I welcome your attentions."

He raised himself up on one elbow and went back at her. "Ever since your sister got married, you have been envious of everything she has. You're being a damn silly, immature brat about this. You are killing all the love we had for each other. We have a nice house here. We eat regularly. We pay our bills. What is it that is bugging you?"

"If you call this barn a nice home, you can keep it. I no longer am interested in it. Its a damn dump. So is everything we have."

"Babe, I need you. Please, let's forget that house out there and enjoy life tonight. You can get mad at me tomorrow but tonight, let's take time out for each other," he pleaded.

"I mean it, John. I won't have anything to do with you until you quit your lousy flying business and get into a better paying job," she bluntly told him.

"Look, Babe, flying has been my life since before I met you. You never got hung up on it before. What else can I do if I don't fly?"

"Then I see no future with you from now on. We are through. Roger and Jane have everything. He treats her like a queen. Just what do you offer me in contrast?"

"Martha, do you realize how much better off we are than many other people? Some men are sick, some are laid off from their jobs. Some have a hard time getting up their monthly rent. We do have a beautiful home here."

"Keep it all. Just shove it all up your butt."

"Do you mean to say you won't have any further relations with me?" he demanded.

"I mean exactly that."

"This is my bed and board," he reminded her. "If you are going to continue this, then I suggest you get out of my bed. I can't sleep next to you like this night after night. I love you. I want you now. Either be my wife or get out of my bed."

Martha got up immediately out of the bed taking her pillow with her. She went into the parlor and laid down on the couch. He lay there in bed for a long time attempting the answer to all of this. "Maybe tomorrow she will see the fallacy of all of this and then we can resume our married life."

The next day being Saturday, he got himself up without waking her or the kids. It would be a busy day at the airport with a warm sunny day ahead. He put together his own breakfast. Then he was gone.

He flew hour after hour on his schedule and student after student. Then at 4:00 P.M., he noticed Ruth was on his next flight appointment. When he came into the office to take her aloft, she smiled that warm smile at him and he responded in kind. "She is a real, sweet kid," he perused.

He walked her out to the training plane and gave her a brief inspection of it and then, after the usual preliminaries, they took their respective side by side seats within the tiny cabin. She sat on the left or "pilot" side and he as Instructor sat on the right side.

They took off and headed out over the nearby countryside for a practice session. She had on a pretty dress, sweater, and her black hair hung about her shoulders. She was now learning to make modest banks, climbs, and glides with the power back, and a pleasant smile creased her peaceful face.

They climbed up to an altitude of 3,000 feet as she handled the controls and he felt exhilarated sitting next to her. Many a time he had a female student next to him, high off the earth, and they all got enthralled and romantic about it. He never quite understood why. Today it suddenly occurred to him. Ruth pointed it out to him when she spoke.

"The earth seems so far away. We are alone out here in space as though on a different planet." He peered down at the earth below him and then realized why it should seem so far away to a woman. Just then the plane hit a strata of bumpy air and Ruth flinched. She hastily let go of the controls, fearing she had done something wrong and grabbed at his arm.

"What made you decide to learn to fly, Ruth?" he asked.

"I don't honestly know but I do enjoy being here right now."

Then she turned her warm fetching smile at him. He was so close to her. He was pressed sideways to her lovely body. And him so hard up for a woman. He hoped secretly that Martha would suddenly relax her belligerence to him that night. He needed Martha so much.

He peered at his wrist watch and knew it was time to return to the home airport. He cut back on the throttle, made the landing, and taxied to the flight line. Ruth muttered that she thought the hour flew by so fast. She made an additional appointment for the following Saturday as he signed her log book with its first hour implanted in it.

When John arrived at home that night, his supper was waiting for him but Martha and the kids were out visiting. He warmed his supper over the gas jet topside above the oven. When Martha returned later, she went to bed on the couch.

He donned his pajamas and came into the parlor to scoop her up into his arms and carry her back to bed. She slapped him hard across the face. His face reddened and he had the urge to belt her right back, but he refrained and went back to his room. Legally a woman could get away with hitting a man, but the law saw only evil in a man responding in kind.

CHAPTER | FOUR

The Zenith Flying Service was a comparatively good–sized flying service, operating ten aircraft with three instructor pilots. They also sat up on an airport with about three hundred privately owned aircraft of all types. John was one of three pilots on the payroll, each one being paid the same amount of money.

While the hours were long during the hot summer time, they were compensated during the winter or slack season, being paid the same weekly wage for less time. The rule was make hay while the sun shines.

When the weather was bad or the field closed, they had a day off but the salary was constant. Sometimes John would receive a small tip or gratuity for helping someone obtain his pilot license with extra effort, and this would provide him with a bit extra spending money. But for the most part, his salary had to do. His base weekly pay was $600, amounting to $31,200 per year.

The weeks went by, and the summer season was narrowing down to August. He had to stay at the airport six days per week until 9:00 P.M. at the peak of Daylight Saving time but by August until 8:00 P.M. In addition there was one night a week he would spend until near midnight, checking out someone on night landings or until near midnight on night cross–country flying. Martha never approved of this long summer stint and now, in addition to her economical reasons for being hard on John, she also had a reason to berate him for not being home enough.

On his day off, he would cut the grass about his home or take the kids to an amusement park or on a picnic but his relationship with Martha had reached a standstill. It got so bad that he rather looked forward to seeing Ruth at the airport just to have someone smile at him. There were times he was booked all day at the airport but would see her when he would get a coffee break.

Ruth started waiting for his coffee breaks and planning her own to coincide with his. He readily assumed it was circumstantial. He loved his Martha and had not as yet violated his fidelity to her, and, even as mad as she was at him, he never doubted her fidelity to him. He would just have to bide his time until her anger at him ran its course and then straightened out.

Ruth worked at the airport at the reception counter to handle all flight appointments and collect fees, answer the UNICOM, and also to help Marian in the back office with the bookkeeping. Ruth worked from Monday to Friday 8:00 A.M. to 5:00 P.M.

Ruth had been through a progression of boyfriends and was worldly wise but as yet not too liberal with her favors. At age twenty, she had an ideal of the type of man she was looking for and had decided to wait until he happened along. Somehow she had fallen in love with John Maloney. She really didn't want it that way. He was married, she told herself, and had made up her mind that it would not be to her advantage to lead him on. But just to be with him was all she wanted.

John would always graciously pay for her coffee, and as was his way, he was always polite, holding a door for her or when they were flying together on weekends, he was always eager to converse with her. For all anyone knew, John was presumed to be a happily married man. He never discussed his home problems with anyone, maintaining that the roots of married bliss, like the roots of a tree, should be hidden from view. It was also a sense of pride with him.

It was Monday morning in late August and John's regular day off from flying. He had planned on taking his kids for a swim and picnic. He no longer had Martha in his bed. She had absented herself from his bed for two months now and in place of the parlor couch had moved into the kids' bedroom to sleep in the twin bed of Kelly.

Little Patty was sleeping in the other twin bed. It appeared that Martha was intending to make a permanent deal out of all this. John could tolerate this with his summer flying hours but, come the fall season, things would have to be different.

He rolled out of bed at 9:00 A.M. so as to cut the grass about the house while Martha was to go shopping. Most of the communication between them was through the kids. Even the kids were being hurt by all of this rigmarole. John had made up his mind to one thing though; he would no longer drive them over to Jane's house. They might call him anti–social all they wanted to but since Jane's home and surroundings were the root cause of his marital problems, then to hell with her going over there.

Martha told little Kelly to ask her father where he intended taking them this day. "Dad, where are we going today?"

"Let's go out to Dreamland Park, have a picnic, a swim, and then you kids can ride the amusement rides if you want to."

"Yippie," they shouted in unison.

He cut the grass and fixed a broken shelf in the kitchen and a leaky faucet in the bathroom sink. By that time, Martha had returned with the ingredients for the picnic and began making the sandwiches. By late morning they were on their way to Dreamland Park. Martha would no longer ride in the front car seat with him, preferring to let Kelly sit up there. She sat in the back with little Patty.

They pulled into the confines of the medium–sized amusement park; parked the car; and carried their lunch basket and large thermos, folding chairs, and swimming suits and headed for the large, open–sided pavilion. This was a large roof–covered veranda housing dozens of picnic tables and benches.

Martha spread out a tablecloth and all of the goodies while the kids' mouths' watered. John had always enjoyed these treats in the past, and he relished this one, being with his two lively, beautiful young daughters and their cute ways.

After finishing their picnic spread, they donned their swimming suits in the nearby bath house and headed for the nearby beach. John saw Martha in her white bathing suit, and that genuine old feeling of warmth stirred within him. She seemed just as smooth and well built as ever, he thought as he studied her. If only she would get over that damn stubborn streak of hers. Life was passing them by.

Toward the end of the afternoon, he took the kids on most of the rides, particularly the Merry–Go–Round with its white steeds and calliope. Now it was time to head homeward.

They pulled into Melody Lane just after darkness had fallen. The kids were all tuckered out and went to bed without any fuss. John walked up behind Martha and put his arms about her waist.

"Please, Babe, come back to bed with me tonight. I love you so very much."

"If you love me as much as you say you do, then quit flying and take a better paying position with more lucrative money in it. If you won't the kids and I are going to leave you. This is my final word to you. I'll go home to my mother's house to live. I'll give you two more weeks. That is all."

He stared at her in disbelief. He had hoped in this length of time, she would want to be more compatible, but now. this. He went to bed disconsolately. What could he do other than flying? At his age of thirty–one years, how could a man retrain for something so alien and opposite to being a pilot? Would he sell insurance? Sell cars? Sometimes those guys starved too. Then he fell asleep.

CHAPTER | FIVE

He went off to the airport on Tuesday morning to begin another week of flying. These were the hazy, dwindling days of late August, and summer would soon be drawing to a close. It would mean two hours less of Daylight Saving Time and a bit more time at home.

He was greeted by Ruth enthusiastically. Ruth always silently regarded Monday as a Blue Monday sort of day—the day John did not come to work. Tuesday was the real beginning of the week where Ruth was concerned.

A week later, just after Labor Day, true to her word, Martha Maloney and her two children moved away from Melody Lane. She gathered all of their clothes, their personal belongings and—borrowing one of her sister's three cars—she moved all three of them to her mother's house, miles away. She left no note.

It was early September and the kids would be starting in school at a new district, Kelly into fourth grade and Patty in the second grade.

John pulled into his driveway late that evening after a night passenger sight-seeing flight over New York City. His house was dark, the front door locked, and no supper available. An enthusiastic but curious neighbor woman came over to verify what John had suddenly suspected.

"Your wife and children moved away, John. She went off to her mother's to live. What are you going to do now? You poor man. Can I give you some supper?"

"No thank you. I'll manage," he wryly answered.

He was not about to go after her. She made the decision and, damn it, now he wouldn't give up flying for her or anybody else. She could stay at her mother's until hell froze over. He looked about the empty house. It was kind of small, he admitted, but what could he do about it other than to rob a bank. The bureau drawers were emptied of all their contents. Most of the kids' personal toys were gone, and suddenly he felt very much alone and let down. He went out to a diner to get a hot meal under his belt and then, near midnight, he returned to his empty house.

He would have to send her money toward their support each week now, and it was going to an even harder ordeal trying to keep up this house and utilities and maintain himself and still give her sufficient money each week for her and the two girls. Well, that was life. Always a kick in the tailpipe.

About a week went by and there was still no contact from Martha. John then called her mother to see if he could still see the kids on Monday, his day off. He sought also to leave part of his paycheck there. Martha's mother, Mae Livingston, answered the phone.

"Yes, John, stop by this afternoon. They will be home from school after 3:00 P.M. The girls do so much want to see you. I hope you understand that all this is not my doing. Jane and I have tried to convince Martha that her place is with you and that is your livelihood. Do come over."

John went over that afternoon to see his two young daughters and leave part of his pay there. He did not see Marsha. She arranged not to be home when he stopped by. Mrs. Livingston was a widow and now bereft of her two married daughters. She resided in a big old–fashioned seven–room house. She was, as always, very courteous. Disconsolately he later returned to his own home.

Melody Lane. How romantic it sounded when first they moved onto this street. Melody Lane, hah. Dreary Lane would sound more appropriate, he thought.

The next day, Tuesday, it rained torrents of moisture and no flying took place. He did not know what to do with himself. He could not stand that empty house, so he elected to hang around the airport until noontime, gabbing with several pilots, and then had lunch with Ruth. He did not let on to her of his personal sorrow.

"Where do most of you single guys hang out at night?" he inquired.

"Here and there," was the answer. "The Kit–Kat Club is a going joint. Lots of action. Why?"

That evening John elected to take in a movie. The picture: "Buffalo Jim." He donned a clean white shirt and gray slacks and headed by himself for a downtown movie house. Standing at the cashier's window by himself, he was suddenly accosted by two good–looking girls on their way into the same show. One of them was Ruth.

When first she saw John, her face lighted up. Until that moment, it was going to be a dull night out for the girls.

"Hello, Ruth. Fancy meeting you here."

"John, so this is the kind of movie you go to see?" she asked. "Is this your night out alone?" He did not answer her. Instead he walked in with both girls and subconsciously followed them to the center of the theater where the three of them found seats together.

When the three of them came out of the movie, he offered to buy them coffee and cake but the one girl declined.

"I really have to get home early tonight. But why don't you and Ruth go have something. Since she knows you, can you see her home?" Ruth looked askance at John.

"How about it, Ruth. Can I see you home?"

Ruth's face beamed; her answer was apparent. So the other girl bid them both a good night and drove home alone. John showed Ruth to his car and helped her into it. He did feel conscious–stricken about it, but what the hell, he really didn't intend to get involved.

"Let's stop off at a diner, Ruth."

"Fine with me, John."

He pointed his car down the highway to a diner where the staff would not know of him and pulled onto the parking lot. They found their way to a booth and had cake and coffee.

"Do you come out alone much, John?"

He looked at her and figured it was time for an honest answer.

"I'm afraid my wife has left me for good, Ruth. She took our two kids and moved into her mother's house. My wife does not approve of my flying for a livelihood so now I don't know what to do for myself."

He led her out to his car and headed for the nearby suburban town where she lived. He parked in front of her house and led her to the doorway. He made no attempt to kiss her and she was glad he didn't. He was still married with children and even though she did enjoy the evening near him, there were still some conscious–stricken realities here.

"See you tomorrow," he said and then left.

CHAPTER | SIX

The days at the airport mounted into weeks and it became very apparent that Martha was committed to staying away. Every Monday John would stop at Mrs. Livingston's and see his two adorable little girls after school hours. He saw no sign of Martha on any of his visits. As far as he knew, she had simply retired from life. Mrs. Livingston was very kind and sympathetic to him and greeted him each time at her door.

On one such afternoon, he was asked to have a light snack and coffee as Mrs. Livingston had something special to relay to him.

"John, Martha has seen a lawyer. She is filing for divorce. Can you stop her?"

"I can't stop her. If that is what she wants, then let her go through with it. I did my best for her and it wasn't enough. So now I suppose I'll have to sell the house to settle the property division."

"Did you know that Jane's baby died last week? It had pneumonia and they lost it almost overnight," she told him.

"Gee, that is sad and a shock. I hate to hear that. With all that they have, they lose their only child. How are they taking it?"

"Jane is taking it very hard. I don't believe he is though."

John left for home on Melody Lane. "So Jane lost her little one. Would Martha realize now that Jane had lost a precious gift of life? Would she still be envious of her sister? Martha had two beautiful daughters and Jane would be without. Would this wake Martha out of her envy?"

Every Saturday afternoon, John would look forward now to flying with Ruth. She was close to making her first solo flight, and both of them relished the thought of a little celebration when she would accomplish the feat. "I'll let you take me out for a big steak dinner when I solo," she had said to him.

He told Ruth that he momentarily expected to hear of his wife's impending divorce but still John did not conceive that he would want to take Ruth out as steady company. She was only a kid of twenty years old, while he was thirty–one, pushing thirty–two. Sure, he was strong, healthy, robust—but would it be fair to a girl like Ruth for him to pay alimony and still be serious with her? He thought otherwise.

On a Saturday afternoon in late November, John was getting some very good and safe landings from Ruth, the wind was calm, and it seemed the right moment. After several landings in which he did not have to help her, he told her to stop the plane along the taxi strip. He opened the door, giving her last minute instructions.

"How do you feel about going up by yourself?"

She smiled warmly at him. Her exuberance was bubbling over. "Don't forget that big steak dinner, John," she admonished him. Then she took off. He watched her all around the rectangular flight pattern with an eagle eye. Then she came in and made a beautiful landing just in front of him. When she taxied back toward him, he climbed back in. They made their way to the flight line and shut the engine off.

She jumped out of the training plane and gave out with a high pitched scream. "Whhheeeee!" she yelled. It was now traditional to kiss her on the lips. He walked up close to her, took her hand into his, and lightly kissed her. Then both looked longingly at each other. Suddenly he reached for her again, sweeping her into his arms and really kissing her. She snuggled close to him and whined: "Oh, John."

Others rushed forward now to congratulate her and loud yells and laughing surrounded them. It was always a big deal when someone soloed an airplane for the first time in their lives. It was like breaking the bonds of imprisonment, or like a swallow leaving the nest for the first time.

With the termination of Daylight Saving Time and the declining sun setting in the west at 5:30 P.M., John drove his car home to his Cape Cod house. He bathed and shaved and, like a schoolboy going out on his first date, he picked up Ruth at 7:30 P.M. and they drove out some twenty-five miles away where he hoped no one would spot him that might recognize him.

Ruth really looked vivacious that night. She had on a dress that really caressed her body. It was two inches above her knees and on it was a sprig of flowers of a small corsage he had purchased for her.

It had been so long since John had seen that exciting look in the eyes of a female. Were they all "battle-axes" after you married them? Then why not stay single and be excited all the time.

They entered the fashionable restaurant and were seated, at Ruth's request, in a corner. They began with a cordial, and Ruth was alive with conversation this night. In the background, a man played music on a console.

This was not only a date with John tonight but a major celebration for Ruth. Not only that but she detected a very hungry look in John's eyes tonight. The way he kissed her this afternoon. Tremendous anticipation ran through Ruth's veins this night. John would be getting a divorce and, all of a sudden, it was no longer wrong for her to be in love with him.

They left the restaurant, and John took her for a ride into the hills of North Jersey, and he stopped on a height overlooking the lights of a small town.

"Ruth," he spoke, drawing her close to him. "I enjoyed this evening with you. You are a wonderful, personable girl. I believe I could fall in love with you with but little effort. But Ruth, I can only offer you a miserable, frugal existence. Because of this I just can't bring myself to taking you for my advantage. Do you understand?"

"I know all the risks, John. I also know you are devoted to your wife and children. I believe you might even go back to them if she changed her mind. I guess that is why I respect you. You are honest," Ruth sighed.

"Can we be friends without emotional problems?" he asked. "I would certainly enjoy taking you out again but I can't promise you anything up ahead to count on. Right now, I would give anything to hold you in my arms and it might mean I would want you for life but I just can't break the barrier that lays between us at this time."

"Just kiss me and take me home," she pleaded.

He took her into his arms and his hungry lips burned into her warm mouth. His hands grasped her shoulders and it seemed as though he might never let go of her. Then slowly he released her and started up the car. They drove homeward in silence. When they arrived in front of her house, she fled the car and ran in without looking back. Her eyes were wet with tears.

He pointed his car homeward. He was a man now torn between devotion in one direction and a burning desire to continue pursuing this beautiful creature he had inadvertently became enthralled with.

CHAPTER | SEVEN

It was a hazy Thursday afternoon in early December. At 4:00 P.M. A twin–engine privately owned executive aircraft was coming straight in for a landing on Runway 9 to the east. It was on a long approach out of the westward sun. One of the Zenith training planes turned base leg just before entering its own approach for a landing. The small Century training plane had an instructor and a student aboard. They never saw the larger corporate–owned plane out there in the thick haze. Behind this executive aircraft was a bright ball of solar fire.

Just as the twin–engine plane neared the confines of the rectangular flight pattern, the training plane also turned from its base leg into its final approach. Both aircraft collided in the air at 500 feet in altitude and plunged helplessly to the sod. The executive aircraft burst into flames as it hit the ground. Aboard the twin–engine plane were two pilots and three executive businessmen. All five of these men burned to death.

At the same moment, the training plane with its two men aboard plunged down into a nearby farmer's field, killing both men aboard. No one at first was sure who was aboard the training plane. It was readily presumed that maybe John Maloney might be aboard as he was due in at that moment.

Ruth ran from the flight office crying and started running down the runway toward the crash scene at the end of the airport. A car stopped to pick her up. She was overwrought. Fire engines and police cars were racing toward the scene. A call went out for ambulances. Sirens wailed and a host of airport personnel raced to the scene to see what they could do.

"It might be John Maloney in that Zenith plane," someone theorized, and Ruth was beside herself. She hurriedly prayed that by some miracle it would not be John.

Police lines were set up about the nearby fire and crash scene a hundred feet apart. Police were holding back a crowd near the wrecked training plane as aid crews extricated its victims to see if there was any spark of life. Ruth strained trying to learn the identity of the two men aboard the training plane marked with its Zenith Flying Service emblems.

She was visibly crying hard now and trying to reassure herself it wasn't John. After ten minutes at the scene, John arrived by car to see who it was. He had just landed being the next one down after the collision. Ruth turned and saw him.

"John, John. Oh thank God it isn't you." She flew into his arms crying hysterically. He patted her head trying to quiet her down. "Oh, John, I was so frightened."

"Its Joe Miller and his student. They never knew what hit them," one of the field attendants told them.

He knew now that Ruth was in love with him. He had not wanted it to happen this way. She was too nice, too sweet a girl. He couldn't just run out on her either. He thought too much of her to do that. Could it be that he loved her too? It had been so long since his life with Martha.

The sun had already set and he took Ruth in for a drink to get her frayed nerves back to normal. After she calmed down and began to smile again, he bought her supper at a diner. Then he took her for a drive up into the lake country. He stopped in a lonely spot and reached for her, drawing her into his arms.

"Oh, John, when I thought it might be you, I just couldn't stand it. I felt my life ending at that moment. Hold me tight."

He held her tightly in his arms, stroking the back of her head with his hand and soothing her. It felt so wonderful to be needed again. Just to feel so necessary to a beautiful girl like Ruth raised his ego from its very low point it had descended to these past few months. But what could he honestly do for her? He suddenly felt a very strong responsibility toward her. He reminded himself he had two young daughters. He knew he could be very happy with Ruth if only he was devoid of his own responsibilities.

Why did life present these rash problems with seemingly no answers to them? What should he do at this point in time? His intuition told him to make tracks backward but he could not do that. Ruth wasn't just a carefree dame. She was someone he valued as a sincere friend. He fully respected her. Circumstances had pushed her into his life. If only Martha had not left him.

He swung Ruth around so that she lay across his lap and in his arms. Within his arms, he kissed her fondly and became intoxicated with her warmth, the feel of her well compressed body, so alive in his arms. The sweet perfume of her being sent wave after wave of heat and passion through him.

He could not let her go. He had never felt so stirred up in his life. She clung so tightly to him. Her affection for him was unlimited. At this point in a relationship, a rogue would have moved in for the kill. He would not. He now loved her so much that only her total security mattered to him.

They clung there motionless for over an hour. The only sound was his heavy breathing and her sighing. He made no move to possess her other than to hold her tenderly close. Then finally he forced him to a conclusion.

"Ruth, this will have to be the last time we see each other like this. It is not fair to you, Ruth. I hate myself for letting it happen. I can offer you nothing in exchange for your love. I want you to seek the company of another from now on. I'll see you at the airport but this will have to be the last time we go out together."

"John, please, don't push me away. I love you. I'll wait for you but don't push me away." She started crying all over again.

"I know now that I love you, Ruth. But it has to end. I'm in a quandary as to what to do. With me you would have a long struggle in a cheap flat at what I will have left for a livelihood. Ruth, seek someone else."

He pointed the car homeward and then changed course for the airport where she left her car that morning. She silently got into her car without looking back at him. Once behind the wheel of her own car, she burst out crying uncontrollably. John drove away, not realizing the full pain he had bestowed upon her.

Friday morning, the day after the horrible accident, Ruth called in sick. It was the first time she had ever reported in sick since she took the position there. John was in a somber mood as well and the pall of the fatal crash hung about the airport. Marian filled in for Ruth that day. Joe Miller had been flying for Zenith a short while but was well liked.

Some of the staff had been familiar with the two pilots flying the late executive aircraft but Miller was their more familiar figure. John had always been a fatalist about such things. In the recent Gulf War, he had managed to keep his wits about him whenever any of his buddies had been shot down. It had to be that way. When your time came to depart this world, you went and not before. Life went on regardless of who you were.

He wondered if Martha really meant her divorce action or if she was bluffing. What concerned him most was the welfare of his two dear little girls. What honest charge could she use in her action. He had not strayed while married to her. He had provided her with a comfortable living and her own home. Could she possibly get a divorce? What would happen to the welfare of his kids? Also, in any divorce action, the house would have to be sold. Yet he dare not sell it now as she might change her mind.

The flying days were now shorter with darkness precluding appointments at 5:00 P.M. Now, after a substantial supper at a nearby diner, it was 6:00 P.M. when he arrived at home. Not too much chance to be lonely but his house was quiet. It was just those heavy rainy or snowy days that bugged him.

Ruth was flying solo lately, piling up practice landings for the day when John would take her out on cross–country, navigational trips. So when Saturday afternoon would arrive, she went into the air by herself and he missed seeing her. He did note her name on the appointment book. By the time he had come back from a charter flight to Albany New York, Ruth had come and gone.

Sunday was another uneventful day at the airport but so busy that he had little time for coffee and a snack. On Monday, his day off, he got up leisurely and, in the middle of the afternoon, made his way over to the Livingston home to see the little ones after their school hours.

Mrs. Livingston greeted him at the door. "Hello, John, come on in. How about a cup of coffee before you take the girls for a ride."

"How is everybody, Jane included?" he inquired then settled himself down on a kitchen chair. Mae Livingston had always been good to him and in spite of his marital difficulties, he could still confide in her and vice versa, even though she was his mother–in–law.

"Martha left for Reno, John. She is getting a 'quickie' divorce from you out there. Jane and I tried to talk her out of it but she is adamant. So I suppose you will be notified when she returns," Mrs. Livingston told him.

"Just like that," John moaned. "Ten years of married bliss terminated on a whim. Does she plan on remaining here with you along with our kids?"

"We have room for them but we are not encouraging it. I believe she has met someone in the last week or so. She has been going out several nights a week. I really shouldn't tell you this."

"We had what I thought was a wonderful marriage but she never seemed to appreciate anything. I worked long hours, but she never gave me credit for anything. There seemed little affection. Then Jane got married. As soon as Jane came into all that fabulous security and big, beautiful home, it suddenly killed our marriage. I'm shocked at the turn of events. She is just filled with envy over Jane and what she came into."

He took his two lively little rascals out for supper, ice cream, and a couple of candy bars and then returned them to Grandma Livingston.

Tuesday morning he awoke and sat quietly on the edge of his bed. He was bewildered at the turn of events. Everything he had believed in was now shattering like a plate of glass. His days even within his house were now numbered. The law would demand that all community property be divided equally between them. Yet he could not dispose of the property until he heard from her lawyer.

He got up and made his way to the bathtub. After that he dressed and walked through the stilled house. He made some last–minute attempts to keep the house clean. He washed out a few dishes that had accumulated, stowing them back into the kitchen cabinet. He put the almost empty garbage can out to the curbstone.

He then drove listlessly toward Sky Harbor Airport and his flying job at Zenith. The days were shorter, and Christmas was a day away. He gathered presents for his girls, for Mae Livingston, and one for Ruth Reynolds. He wondered what he might do with his life from now on. He couldn't leave this area. He wanted to stay near his kids. They were an integral part of his life. You didn't divorce yourself from your children. And flying—much as he tried to deny it—was his life.

CHAPTER | EIGHT

John walked into the airport flight office amid the usual hail fellow and other friendly diatribes from his co–workers. They were always a warm group. It was just another Tuesday morning, the beginning of another flying week for him. Ruth saw him coming and then pretended to ignore him.

"Good morning, Ruth. How are you?" he asked.

Ruth did not answer but turned her attention to the rest of the gang. Since he had made it plain that he thought it best to remain distant from her and since she felt she had made a fool being previously so close to him, she was going to pry him out of her system.

In his present state of melancholy, he was glad to note that he was down on the schedule for a charter trip to Richmond, Virginia. He didn't feel like a lot of gabbing with students this day. He asked Ruth for a weather report. She relented her coolness, glad now that he was talking to her.

"High overcast, snow and fog moving in by early this evening. You are to pick up the Simpson couple at Richmond and get them home in time for a social engagement this evening," Ruth answered. She eyed him up and then gave vent to her inner feelings. "You better watch the weather, John."

He nodded agreement and then touched her arm with his hand reassuringly, though he hadn't meant to do so. She watched him go out the door toward the powerful Skyline aircraft. After taking on full tanks and an additional quart of oil, he started the engine up, whirling the propeller about. He taxied to the end of Runway 9. The wind was blowing from the Northeast at 15 M.P.H., a very positive indication of impending snow, what with the anticipated dropping in temperature.

He took off and turned the airplane southward toward Philadelphia, climbing to the height of 4,000 feet enroute. Subsequently he flew past Baltimore, Maryland, to the eastern side of Washington D.C., and then followed the railroad tracks leading toward Richmond Virginia. At noon, he landed at Byrd Field and waited in the terminal building. The weather in the area was sunny and mild.

The Simpsons were used to making people wait, as they were loaded with money. Cost was no object. John announced his arrival over the phone to the homestead where they were staying and after being told that they would be delayed for a period of time, he headed for lunch at a nearby restaurant.

He had the plane topped off with full fuel tanks, giving him a fresh range of distance for over four hours time and then waited in the terminal building at Byrd field. Shortly after 2:00 P.M., the Simpsons arrived by limousine with their baggage. John loaded them aboard the 220 H.P. Skyline aircraft. He glanced up at the sky that had changed from sunny and mild to a high overcast as it had been earlier in North Jersey.

The trip back home even with its headwind would not consume more than two and a half hours, he estimated. With a bit of God–given luck, he would beat the weather. Aviation was still a gamble but wasn't all of life a gamble? Even love had its challenges, he thought.

Once aloft with Mr. and Mrs. Simpson, he sought to play down the weather angle but tuned into a Vortac Station to hear the weather reports enroute northward. It was already snowing in Hartford, Connecticut; Albany, New York; and the eastern part of Long Island. Low scud was moving southward toward him. The snowline was as reported, still seventy–five miles above Sky Harbor, his home base.

He cleared the Washington D.C. area without a flight plan and preferred to stay on VFR (visual flight rules), the visual, unreported way of flying. There was always too much air traffic on the IFR (instrument flight rules) and conversing with different air controllers and the much re–routing that would delay him if he filed such a plan.

At Baltimore, the overcast had dropped down to 2,000 feet above sea level with occasional scud as low as 800 feet. He maintained the 2,000 with visibility at 4 miles forward.

At Philadelphia, 90 miles from home base, visibility had dropped to 2 miles forward and a ceiling down to 800 feet. The trip to home base would not be no more than forty minutes.

He latched onto the New Jersey Turnpike because, as the ceiling would decline, he had a perfect visual concrete beam by riding atop it.

Back at Sky Harbor, it had already started with light snow. Visibility went down to two miles and the ceiling, at best, to 500 feet. All the aircraft at home base were in and secured. Ruth stayed close to the telephone atop her counter and to the UNICOM receiver and microphone. She was waiting to her whether John had landed elsewhere or was still roaring northward.

As the time wore on past her normal quitting time, she became anxious. Marian, nearby, suggested to Ruth that she go over to the snack bar for a Coke, but at that moment nothing was going to pry her out of the office.

John reached a point along the Jersey Turnpike when he felt he was moving too fast at his 150 M.P.H. airspeed to properly focus on his landmarks below him.

He changed his propeller pitch to a power setting, giving him a far lower cruising speed but more of a power ratio. He lowered partial flap adding to his drag so he could better feel his way above the highway. He then had slowed down from 150 M.P.H. to an airspeed of 100 M.P.H. His visual ceiling was now 600 feet and starting to snow. He crossed the Raritan River and figured he could still make it to home base.

While following the Turnpike, he decided to call the UNICOM at Sky Harbor and alert them that he was indeed on his way in and asked if they would have a taxicab standing by for the Simpsons.

"Sky Harbor Unicom, Skyline 7745 Temple. What is your ceiling and visibility there?"

Ruth quickly recognized that he was calling in and she lunged for the microphone. "Sky Harbor Unicom to Skyline 7745 Temple. Visibility here is 1,000 feet ahead, with snow. Ceiling only a bare few hundred feet. Where are you, John?" she asked excitedly.

Others groped within the Flight Office listened in stony silence. "That son–of–a–gun is going to make it in this? Here?"

The runway lights were put on and the revolving beacon went on in the gathering twilight. Ruth clung to the radio communication set with mike in hand. She wasn't about to let go of it to anyone else.

John reached the Newark area where the Turnpike crossed the northbound Garden State Parkway, and now he glued the airplane onto the Parkway as it proceeded close to his destination. The next fifteen minutes would be highly crucial to him.

Ruth called him again over the UNICOM with heavy apprehension in her voice. "Sky Harbor Unicom to Skyline 7745 Temple; where are you now, John?"

"Skyline 7745 Temple, am just over Orange. Will be in within ten minutes. Take it easy, Ruth."

She smiled wanly; he never got excited over anything. Sometimes she could kill that lug up there.

John reached a road heading westward that crossed under the Parkway but ran through the Orange Mountains. It would take him to his airport. Pilots from other States were always kidding him about the so–called Orange Mountains. They were anthills compared to other mountains, they would tell him. But today, those 700 foot mountains were higher than the plane he was flying. He wished he didn't have to go through them.

He was now at 400 feet above this west–pointed road, and if he stayed just above it, he could squeak right through the pass. The first one suddenly loomed right up in front of him. He roared through, scaring the daylights out of people just 100 feet below him with his thunderous aircraft. Then the next pass loomed up and he made this one in a fast buzz job just above the telephone wires.

Then the road dropped back down a couple hundred feet below him again. A minute later, he reached the perimeter of the airport and recognized a hangar line. Heavy snow was now pounding against his windshield and wings. His defroster provided but a diminishing circle of clear forward vision. He realized if he had to fly much longer, the snow in the windsheer of his speed would freeze and load him heavily with the burden of ice.

"Sky Harbor, I'm here above you and coming in now. I see the beacon...keep the coffee hot."

Ruth and the others dropped what they were doing now and rushed to the windows. They couldn't see much of anything but all of a sudden, a loud roar went over the top of the office and then he was gone. He slowed the plane down to 80 M.P.H. as he banked around trying to find the beginning of Runway 9. Intuitively he groped for some visual part of it. Then he caught a shimmering temporary glimpse of it at 200 feet up, with the snow hammering at his windshield giving him a white–out at his speed.

He touched down at 65 M.P.H. A squeal of his tires was heard in the already inch–deep snow on the ground, and then he groped his way slowly toward the flight office. As he pulled up, and someone opened the hangar doors, allowing him to pull right into the hangar without getting his passengers wet.

He shut down the engine and took a temporary quick breath. After the Simpsons were helped out of the plane and paid their tab, they got into the cab.

The airport collected for six hours of flight time and two hours of waiting time. Mr. Simpson stuffed a $50 bill in John's hand as a tip. "Good, safe trip," he smiled. Out of the corner of his eye, he saw Ruth's anxious face nearby.

When he went into the office, Marian started to kid him. "John, why don't you forget those hair–raising entrees. You scared the daylights out of poor Ruth here. I had to hold her up. She worries more about you than all the rest of us put together. What have you done to our little girl?" Then she laughed.

"You weren't worried, were you, Ruth? It was just another flight."

Ruth was petulant. She glared at him with a mixture of anger and tears. "I hate you, John."

It was now time for all of them to make tracks for home in the growing threat of a worsening snowstorm. John walked over to Ruth and attempted to cajole her. "How about supper with me, Ruth?" he asked.

"No, John. I have a new boyfriend now. He is big, mean, jealous, and better looking than you and he carries a big gun. So you better run while you are able to."

He smiled at her. Then he grasped her arm and squeezed it. It was body language. It was affection. Then he turned and went out toward his car. She peered after him with misty eyelids and a sniffle.

CHAPTER

NINE

The day's mail brought John the official legal notice of Martha's divorce action. If he wished to contest it, there was a time limit of thirty days. Her charge was incompatibility, the only option open to her. If there was no contest, he was requested to meet with her lawyer and work out some financial arrangements.

He did not contest the action and indicated that he wished to cooperate with the proceedings without further legal aid on his part. "These lawyers cost money," he reasoned. There were numerous cases in which the lawyers grabbed all the available money, leaving none to those involved as either plaintive or defendant.

He put his house up for sale and it was sold within a week. All the furniture was sold to a used furniture dealer and odds and ends sold to neighbors or friends. His car was listed as an asset but in lieu of some of the house money, he kept the car. After the house was sold, the balance principal of the mortgage was paid.

The money he had invested into the house, plus its rise in inflationary value, produced the clear sum of $82,000 clear. Out of this the legal fees were paid and he and Martha divided the rest, with her receiving $35,000 and he, in lieu of keeping his car, received $30,000. He agreed to her custody of the children with visitations rights for himself. He agreed to support payments of $150 per week as he had voluntarily paid previously.

He then took his share of the money, and after extracting half the sum for himself, he put the other $15,000 into a trust fund for the kids to draw from as they each would reach the age of twenty–one. The trust fund for his kids would be guarded by the bank. This trust fund for his two little girls was his own idea and not the idea of the lawyer involved.

He then obtained a small furnished room with a bath for himself. After packing his clothes and personal effects, he left Melody Lane for the last time. He notified Zenith Flying Service of his change of address and telephone number, and Ruth inadvertently learned his divorce was final, just like that.

Ruth did start going out on dates with other men—and with one man in particular but her heart belonged to John, and she knew it could not change. There were now other forces at work in the strange pattern of destiny in John's life. All of life is an intricate pattern of ongoing interloping results that no human being can either control or design for himself. Destiny is but the hand of God.

John figured if he was to create a new life for himself, it would have to be with new resources and not those that might otherwise belong to his kids. He felt that he owed Martha nothing further at this point in time but his kids were the innocent pawns of the circumstances. He also changed the beneficiary of his insurance to his kids.

On Sunday afternoon at the airport, a young student pilot, up solo flying to build flying time on his landings, was having difficulty trying to land one of the Century training planes in a sudden crosswind landing. Confused by the intricacies of the wind, he over–controlled the plane, sending it slamming into the runway sideways and bounding up into the air about twelve feet high.

Once again he hit the ground with a severe wallop and, in trying to recover, he hit the throttle full on and decided to go around the flight pattern for another attempt to land. His Instructor raced into the flight office to talk to him over the UNICOM and try to help him.

"Sky Harbor Unicom to Century 2202 Zulu. Let me talk you in on your next landing. Keep it cool, calm down."

"Century 2202 Zulu to Zenith. Go ahead I read you."

"Smitty, listen carefully. Make the same approach as you did before but keep trying to keep your left wing down and into the wind. Keep your fuselage straight by walking your rudder.

"Walk your rudder. Don't let that left wing up except to level off. Then left wing down again. Ignore the bumpy air."

Once again the training plane came in on its final approach and was bouncing around in one of those situations that have long been the nemesis of the unwary student pilot. He set up his approach–line to the runway while the Instructor in the flight office talked him in.

The training plane was almost ready to settle to the runway in its full stall landing. Then he instinctively leveled his wing, causing it to accept more lift on its wing and suddenly ballooning up once more to twelve feet high.

The student inadvertently shoved the control wheel forward, and 2202 Zulu crashed on the runway. The nose wheel sheared off the plane. The propeller twisted into a pretzel, and one wing was slightly damaged.

The student was uninjured except for his ego. He escaped as usual in a light plane accident but the damaged aircraft had to be towed off the runway for serious repairs. It was fated to be that this accident to this particular plane would ultimately change the course of John's future life.

Once again it was a Monday afternoon. The kids were due out of school at 3:00 P.M. John was itching to see them and see if they needed anything. Mae Livingston phoned him and asked him to come over for lunch before the kids would come home. The girls were now one year older. Kelly was ten years of age and Patty was eight years of age. They were growing up.

"John, how are you? Come in and sit with me. I want to confide in you," she said.

"Hello, Mother, what's new?" he asked.

"I regret very much the break–up of your marriage. I'm afraid it is punishing us all," she started. "Martha is going with some wealthy architect who she claims will marry her now that she is divorced. I haven't met him yet but from what I see of the situation and the way she meets him clandestinely, I don't like what's going on. I get the impression he is just using her."

"It's her life from now on," John said. "Frankly I don't care anymore what she does but I am glad the kids are here with you. I feel comfortable about that. I couldn't possibly take care of them and still make a living. It's Martha's turn now to find the things she wants from life. I wish her the best. I paid my dues. It's her ballgame now."

"John, I think Jane and her husband are about to break up. Since the death of her baby, he goes away on weekends on his own. He claims it is all part of his law business. She found out that he is transferring his funds and stocks out of the local banks and has cut way down on her house money."

"You mean to say that with all that supposed security that Jane, had and the way Martha envied her, that Jane now may lose it all? That is very sad and ironic to me," he replied.

"Jane thinks Roger is getting ready to discard her for another woman. They haven't had much to do with each other since their baby died. She also read in the gossip column that Roger met and has been seen with that sensational new movie actress, Blaze Furey. He supposedly is handling her legal representation. He is just a playboy, and now he is about to unload Jane for his next conquest."

"That's a nasty shame. Jane is a very beautiful girl," John allowed. "I hope she makes out all right."

Mae Livingston continued: "I believe Martha in time will regret her actions. Right now she only has materialistic aims. I'm worried about both of my daughters. Martha goes off for a few days at a time and just assumes that I will raise her little ones. The poor dears are so confused about the drift of their parents.

"You know, John, Ken and I never had these problems. We had our tough times too, but we were always there for each other. The only divorces back then concerned millionaires and those in the entertainment industry. Now the divorce rate has ballooned up to 60 percent, and it is all a disgrace. Ken and I lived in a cold water flat. He worked for a machine shop but never made much money. One night he told me if he had the money, he would love to open up his own machine shop. He devised a few inventions. I started waiting on tables with nickel and dime tips to help him gather enough to get started. Then we made out very successfully and were able to buy this house while our two girls were still youngsters. Ken left me well provided for when he passed away. People were more dedicated to each other back then."

Shortly after 3:00 P.M. the two girls were home from school, and John grabbed them up in his arms. They laughed and showered their father with hugs and kisses. It was highly important to show them that regardless of the status of his old married life, he still cherished his darling little girls. Martha was careful to avoid him on Mondays. She always made a point to be out when he called.

John drove back to his furnished room deep in thought. He now had some money in the bank from the divorce action and a few dollars spending money. He would have to support his kids for several years into their future or at least till the youngest left school and secured a position. It left him little money to recklessly squander. Money for his room, meals, a few clothes, and car expenses. Maybe Martha was right. What kind of a future could he offer to another woman at this point. Money wasn't everything but it sure could solve a lot of problems.

CHAPTER | TEN

When he went to the airport the next morning, Ruth greeted him once again with her big warm smile. In fact, it appeared she was in a rare mood this day.

"Good morning, Ruth. Boy, do you look gorgeous in that outfit," he greeted her. She was a peppy, voluptuous humdinger this morning.

"Hi, John. A busy day ahead for you. But I blocked off 1:00 P.M. for you so you can have lunch, and you are going to treat me to lunch today. That suit you?"

He looked at Ruth and smiled. He liked the way she could wrap him around her finger. She sure had a winsome way about her. "Okay, you got a date," he smiled.

Shortly after 1:00 P.M. and his busy morning and long flight schedule, John landed with his student. After signing his logbook and re–scheduling him for another appointment, he and Ruth strode over to the airport snack bar for lunch. This time Ruth steered him into a booth. There were some things she wanted to discuss with him.

"John, I see you have a new address and phone number now," she opened with.

"Yes, Ruth, I'm divorced now and am now a free, poor, but proud man."

"When are you going to ask me out again?" she persisted.

"Ruth, I would really love nothing better than to take you out. Do you want to know what you are in for? I have seventy–five dollars a week for my meals after all other expenses. What kind of a future can I offer a young girl like you?"

"I'm willing to share expenses with you if you are willing."

"What about your other male interests? A gal like you must be pretty well booked with some very eligible young men."

"I have a fellow I'm going with who insists he wants to marry me, but I can't ever love him. He just isn't it. Now that you are divorced, I won't be wrong in going out with you. As far as costs, you have always been honest about things, so I know what I'm getting into."

"Do you also know how old I am?"

"You sure do think up a lot of ways to discourage a girl. You are now thirty–two years old, right? Now can we have a date?"

"You win," he smiled. "When do I walk the plank?"

"Will you take me out this Friday night? I'll wear my new dress, and we can go dancing at the Westmount Club. Okay? You know, John, Sunday is my birthday but I want to start celebrating it with you. I'll be twenty–one next Sunday."

All of a sudden, John had something to look forward to. It would be wonderful to take out this beautiful doll.

All day Friday, Ruth was bubbling over with enthusiasm. Everyone who ventured into the flight office could not fail to notice how happy and carefree she was. Each time John came in with a student, her eyes would light radiantly as he in turn watched her with that wonderful glow that a man has for a beautiful creature.

They had a fast cup of coffee during the day but it was the coming date that evening that both of them relished. By now Marian and the rest of the crew of Zenith Flying Service knew that John Maloney had been recently divorced and was the aggrieved party. It was also recognized that Ruth Reynolds had a terrific crush on him but no one really knew whether he was dating her yet. It just wasn't anyone's business.

As John finished up his day of flying at 6:00 P.M., he rushed home to bathe and change into his best suit and tie. In most cases when a man like John dated a girl, it was for a mutual accommodation. Not with John. He already thought enough of Ruth to want only the best of any situation for her. He would enjoy just being with her this night.

He drove out to her house with a small corsage and, all of a sudden, he was a young, high–spirited kid again. He rang the doorbell, and her mother admitted him. Ruth was the youngest of her three children and the last of the three to leave home for wedlock. Ruth was the baby of the family.

"Hello, John. I've heard so much about you from Ruth. I almost feel I know you. So you are a pilot at her airport. Well, now you be careful, both of you."

Presently Ruth made her appearance in her new dress that was just above her knees but with a flair hemline to it, and she looked ravishingly attractive. He handed her the corsage. Her mother thought to herself that Ruth appeared more alive than ever before in her life. This guy John must be the one about whom her daughter really cared.

He led her out to his car and opened the door for her. She climbed in, and he shut the door after her. As he took his place behind the steering wheel and started off, it was with a feeling of trepidation and pride. Ruth was bubbling over with vivaciousness tonight, and he had a treasure beside him.

They drove into the parking lot of the Westmount Club and surrendered the car to a parking valet. Then they proceeded into the dining hall where the headwaiter guided them to a corner table. John ordered a canter of wine and then dinner.

While awaiting the entree, Ruth asked to dance. He led her out onto the dance floor and took her into his arms. Then he realized what he had been missing all of his life. Never before had he felt as happy as he did at that moment. Her face, her form, and her personality were glued to him as though she had been born next to him.

He felt like a very young swain again. Ruth fit snugly close to him. Her eyes reflected the pleasure she felt in the arms of this tall, soft–spoken man whom she had long admired. After several dances, both retired to their table and began eating.

"John, I have eight hours of solo flying time, and in just two more weeks you are going to have to teach me cross–country flying. So be prepared. I want to go down to Atlantic City on my first trip with you, okay?"

"You mean you will have your ten hours of solo flying in just two more weeks? Well, you see, I usually make three cross–country trips with a student. Two trips to help him and the third trip they have to prove they can reach their destination and get home themselves without any help from me. Think you can handle all of that?" he grinned.

"I'll be raring to go, John. To Atlantic City."

"Why don't we wait till September for Atlantic City when Miss America will be down there. Then I can bring her home with me," he gloated.

"I'll give you Miss America. I'll wring your big bull neck," she laughed.

They ate and they danced; then it was time to head for home. He parked his car at the darkened airport parking lot on their way homeward. They embraced and kissed. Then his hands began to roam. She abruptly stopped him.

"No, not that," she begged him.

"Well, just let me hold you then," he pleaded. He swung her around so that she lay across his lap. Her knees doubled up and her open–toed shoes pressed tightly against the car door. Never before in all his life had he felt the need for a girl as he did for her at that tender moment.

She was without a doubt the epitome of all of his future happiness if only he could straighten out his economic problems and his responsibility to his youngsters. The quiet warmth and electronic contact between them was no temporary, spur–of–the–moment infatuation. He realized inwardly that Ruth was what he now wanted if only....

"We had better go now, John. You have to fly tomorrow."

He took her home; dropped her off at her house and headed back to his lonely, dingy, furnished room. Ruth's mother greeted her as she came in the door.

"Ruth, you look so happy. Is John the one in which you really are interested?"

"Yes, Mother. He is the one. I'm going to marry him, only...he doesn't know it yet. But he will," she giggled.

After a busy flying weekend, John had another day off and used it to visit his kids. He would arrive at his former mother–in–law's home in the early afternoon about lunchtime. He would do some necessary shopping or go to a coin–operated laundry in the late morning.

"Hello, John," Mae Livingston would greet him. "Did you have your lunch yet? Come on in and have coffee and a sandwich."

"Hello, Mother. How's the kids?" After they sat down she would bring him up to date on the current news.

"John, Roger and Jane are getting divorced. He is doing the so–called proceeding. He is trying to get her out of that house, and he accuses her of just about everything. I just don't know what has happened to our family. I used to think that both of my daughters did so well marrying the boys." Mrs. Livingston began to cry. "Now all of you are breaking up."

"That's too bad about Jane. I am so sorry about that. I read Roger is reported having a whirlwind romance with that movie queen, Blaze Furey. But that won't last. Jane deserves much better than that ham. I just hope he settles generously with Jane. I think it all began with Martha's envy of Jane though. The jealousy and envy for Jane's temporary goods killed our marriage."

"That architect had promised to marry Martha. Now he just puts her off. He isn't going to marry her. She has made a big public fool of herself. Why don't you take her back, John, and rebuild your marriage? She needs you so much now."

John said nothing but was surprised at the request. He put his head down and did not answer her. Shortly after, the two girls bounded in from school, and he was able to dodge the request outright.

"Daddy, you said you might take us up for an airplane ride. Can we go today?"

"Yes, let's go. We will be back in time for their supper," he promised.

As he entered the flight office, he introduced his little ones to the staff, and they all remarked that he did have two beautiful, well–behaved cherubs in flowery dresses. Ruth's eyes glistened at the sight of these little darlings. Then he took them up for their first ever flight amid their "oh's and ah's." They talked about it all evening.

"Ruth, you haven't flown lately. Tired of it?"

"No, John, but I have run low on money. I used up all my savings. Now I have to save much more. I'll get back to it soon. I can't wait till I make my cross–country trips with you."

CHAPTER | ELEVEN

The hot summer season went by in New Jersey and with it the advent of the fall season. During the summer months when his kids were on their summer vacations, he took them to many resorts and swimming sessions every clear Monday. A few times, he included their grandmother, Mae Livingston, as that woman was so vitally important to the raising and general welfare of these kids.

Mae Livingston always enjoyed her outings to Dreamland Park as well as trips to the seashore. As she herself said: "I really haven't enjoyed life as much as I enjoy these day trips with John and the children."

Monday at Sky Harbor Airport was always a dull day as far as Ruth was concerned. Yet she could draw some benefit out of it. She could concentrate more on her required duties. It was on this particular Monday that she heard a chance remark from the president of Amalgamated Pharmaceutical Corporation that his chief pilot on his executive aircraft fleet was going to retire on the first of November.

Ruth put two and two together. She knew that Amalgamated flew two top–of–the–line business jet aircraft, known as Meteor Aircraft. They employed four pilots, two on each aircraft.

Later on that day, Ruth made a person to person telephone call to this president upon his return to his office.

"Mr. Herlihy, this is Ruth Reynolds at Sky Harbor Airport, here in New Jersey," she began.

"Hello, Ruth, how are you? Say, this is a pleasure talking to you. What might I do for you?"

"Mr. Herlihy, I heard that your chief pilot is going to retire soon—is that true?"

"Why yes, Ruth, that is true but...."

"Mr. Herlihy, you are going to need another pilot on your staff. I have a man here whom I believe is properly qualified to take his place with you. He has had a lot of varied flying experience. He flew jet fighters with the Air Force in the recent Gulf War. He has flown air taxi, charter, flight instruction. He is sober, responsible, reliant, and just right for a place as pilot on your staff. He...."

Mr. Herlihy laughed. He had oft times seen Ruth at the flight desk at Sky Harbor. He knew her slightly for her warmth and friendly, outgoing manner. He had often while airborne heard his pilots in the air receive information over the UNICOM.

"Just a minute, Ruth. If he is all that you say he is, why don't you have him come over to my office tomorrow morning at 10:00 A.M. and I'll look him over. Is he a friend of yours?"

"You may know him. He is John Maloney, and he is a wonderful person. I'll have him see you tomorrow at 10:00 A.M. sharp," she promised.

Mr. Herlihy smiled profusely as he laid his telephone down. A friend of such a beautiful girl as Ruth Reynolds would just have to be interesting to meet to say the least. He quickly marked John's name onto his appointment book for the next morning.

Ruth then waited until she finished her work at 5:00 P.M. She then made it a point to intercept John at his boarding house that evening. She sat there from 7:00 P.M. to 8:00 P.M. outside the door of his place to prepare him for his next day's meeting and interview.

At 8:00 p.m., she got out of her car at the sight of him parking his car and related the news of his next day's appointment.

"John, I had to come here to tell you that you have an interview with Mr. Herlihy tomorrow morning at 10:00 A.M. He is looking for another pilot on his staff. He wants to see you, John. Will you go and look into it? Its your big chance, John. He is paying big salaries...."

"Boy, that sounds good. How come he wants to see me?"

"He has probably heard all about your experience, John. He is looking for a capable pilot, that is all."

"Thank you, Ruth. I'll be there." He then walked her back to her car, and she kissed him lightly on the cheek for luck.

He got up early, bathed, and dressed, wondering what fortunate break might possibly be coming his way that morning. He pointed his car toward the New York City main office of the Amalgamated Pharmaceutical Corporation. He arrived a bit ahead of time at the fifteenth floor suite and was ushered into the inner office of Mr. Herlihy's private secretary.

"Good morning. I have an appointment with Mr. Herlihy at 10:00 A.M.," he began.

"All right, kindly take a seat for a few moments," the secretary asked. She called the inner office and in seconds ushered John within.

"Mr. Maloney, come on in and take a seat. I've been expecting you." Herlihy began: "I understand you are an ex–Air Force pilot, you flew jet fighters, and have been a flight instructor for the last eleven years."

"Yes sir, I did," John admitted. "I've been flying for the last fourteen years and am looking for a more permanent position as a pilot."

After an hour exploring John's background and being very much impressed with John and his directness, Mr. Herlihy hired John to start work with the firm on November first, about two weeks from that moment. After all the preliminaries, Herlihy offered John the following advantages.

"Our chief pilot leaves us on November first. You will then come on as junior pilot for the fleet. You will be our number four pilot. As each one moves up the ladder in seniority, you too, will move along. You will spend two weeks down in Texas at the Meteor Jet factory getting used to flying this aircraft.

"After that you will work out of our big hangar at Sky Harbor five days a week, Monday to Friday but occasionally on a Saturday. You will start at $50,000. After one year you will receive $65,000. Eventually you will receive $125,000 as Chief Pilot. That suit you?"

"That suits me fine. I really want to thank you for giving me this opportunity," John said as he got up to leave.

"Well now, don't thank me. Actually, I hadn't mentioned to anyone as yet that I needed another pilot. You had better thank Ruth Reynolds for twisting my arm on this. I still don't know how she knew we were going to need another pilot. She's a very cute girl though, and I don't mind her recommending someone. So thank her. In the meantime, drop over to our hangar and introduce yourself to our present crew over there. Goodbye, John."

"Goodbye, Mr. Herlihy, and once more, thank you."

John left New York and headed back to his job at Zenith.

"So it was Ruth who set me up for this new flying job." He smiled happily to himself. Doggone that Ruth, she was always looking out for his interests. Now he would be able to afford things. Maybe he and Ruth might just make a life together after all.

He walked into the Flight Office at 12:30 P.M., Ruth glanced quizzically at him with an expectant smile on her face. He winked at her and nodded. Quickly she broke into the happiest smile he had ever seen. Her whole face became a red beaming lantern.

She ducked over for a fast bite to eat with him as he was scheduled to fly at 1:00 P.M.

"I understand that you got me that job, Ruth. What brand of sorcery do you use?" He told her all the details of this new job and when he would start.

"I'm glad for you, John. Now you will have no excuse for not taking me out."

"How about supper tonight. I think I have enough dough on me."

Ruth looked hurt. "Oh, I have a date with Merle again. He asked me to marry him once more. Tonight he will ask me again."

"Do you love him?"

Ruth stuck her tongue out at him. "No, I don't love him. He's nice though. At least he asks me."

"Don't marry him then."

"Well, I'm getting older each day," she said. "I'm going to be twenty–two years of age. If I wait too long I might be an old maid. At least Merle thinks I'm worth being a wife." She raised her eyebrows at him hoping he would take the hint. She was just a beautiful girl, five foot two inches tall. He just bowed his head.

Toward the end of October, Indian summer prevailed throughout northern New Jersey. The air was getting colder but the skies were mostly sunny. John gave Zenith notice he would be leaving for his new position at the end of the month. Ruth had completed her required ten hours of solo flying, most of which was landing practice, and by Saturday the following week, she was to start her cross–country flying with John.

CHAPTER | TWELVE

It was Monday, his day off, and time once more to visit his beloved little girls who were now a year older. Kelly had turned eleven years of age and Patty, was nine years of age. He had about settled the things that had seemed problematical to him. With his new position in mind, he intended to ask Ruth to marry him. He would soon be able to afford to marry her and put a house and home together once more. Mae Livingston greeted him at the front door.

"Come right on in, John. Grab a seat," she invited.

"Hello, Mother, how are you?" he greeted her warmly.

"John, Martha is here and wants to talk to you. Shall I call her? I do wish you two would go back together." She then called Martha from another room. Martha was dressed in her best dress but John did not fail to see how drawn and haggard she looked lately. Obviously, she had been let down by the man who had used her and was now seeking a way out of the situation.

"John, how are you?" she greeted him. "I'd like to say a few words to you. Mother insists that I discuss our situation and reconcile. How do you feel about it?"

"I'm afraid it is too late, Martha. I am in love with someone else now. I'm sorry, but it just would not work out for you and me anymore."

"So you are in love with someone else, are you!" she screamed at him. "You have a hell of a nerve to say that to me after I gave you ten of the best years of my life."

"Martha, you are the one who broke up our home, not me. You walked out on me. You are the one who wasn't satisfied. You are the one who sought a more prosperous husband than I. I no longer love you the way that I used to. But you yourself killed our marriage, not I."

"John, I have condescended to go back with you on your meager income until such time as you can raise yourself up to a better position in life. I am more than willing to tolerate your flying for another month or two, for the sake of our children," she stormed at him.

"You have already given yourself to another on a vague promise of matrimony and now you expect me to take you back. You seem to forget that you divorced me, and we are no longer man and wife. We are legally divided. You have no bargaining position with me, Martha. You certainly were not thinking of our children when you deserted me." He decided at that moment not to reveal the fact he had of a new position in the offing. She was not entitled to know of it.

"The very least you can do is to provide a decent home for our children. You never thought very much of any of us or you would have been a better provider as was...." Then her voice trailed off.

"As was Roger?" he inquired.

"I will give you one week to make up your mind as to whether we reconcile or not. I shall not wait indefinitely. Your place is with your wife and children. I may have been a bit hasty in divorcing you, but you had it coming."

"Martha, I have sat here listening to you now and I have yet to hear you make any apology or express any regret for your actions and yet you think my love for you can be turned on or off like a hot water faucet. I see no further advantage to living with you. The trust is gone in the wind. You are completely devoid of feeling for anyone but yourself. You are a self-centered, selfish, egotistical woman. You are a spoiled brat who never quite grew up. So don't use our children as a bargaining point with me. It won't work."

At that moment the kids came in from school and rushed into their father's arms. "Oh, Daddy. Are you and Momma going to take us home to live? Oh, Daddy, that will be swell."

A lump formed in John's throat as Martha gloated at him. If he didn't care about her he certainly did for his kids, she reasoned.

"Daddy is going to decide by next week, children."

He took his children out for a ride and bought them some supper and then woefully took them back to the Livingston home. Afterward he drove home despairingly, wondering whether he still was entitled to happiness at his age of thirty-three or whether he should put his own desires aside for his children. Maybe he did owe them some kind of homelife with him and Martha.

His thoughts trailed back to Ruth. What a wonderful, affectionate girl to have to cast aside just to give his kids the life he felt they should have in their formative years. Ruth was always interested in him. He was sure of her love for him. Ruth had gotten him his new, pending position and his new lease on life. What should he do? If he did go back with Martha, he would insist on separate beds. Martha no longer was a true wife to him regardless of how they might remarry.

"Oh, God. What should I do?"

CHAPTER | THIRTEEN

We blase mortals often refer to the great works of God Almighty as nature in process or to the chronicle of events as evolution; or the passing history of life and death as fate or the division of wealth as luck. We seldom publicly allow credit for a blessed chain of circumstances as being decreed beforehand by our Great Creator. But this tormenting problem confronting John Maloney at that moment in time was about to be decided in the higher halls of Heaven.

Thousands of years before the birth of Christ, the great God of us all had set up the process of evolution of phases of development for this planet earth that included the ice age. When the ice age and its glaciers receded, it left in its wake certain physical changes for our present environment.

Along the New Jersey shoreline, there is a vast pattern of sand bars, swamps, islands, and washed out soil upon which no civilization has as yet set up. It is a system of eroded wasteland for which there is as yet no apparent need.

It was this area in league with a chain of events that was to decide the future plans of John Maloney, Ruth Reynolds, Martha Maloney, and their two children. The Farmer's Almanac predicted a week of heavy rain, fog, mist, and a low pressure area for the Eastern Seaboard of the Northeastern states including New Jersey for the first week of November. Daylight Saving Time had precluded and clocks were back to Standard Time with darkness starting at 5:30 P.M.

The maintenance shop of the Zenith Flying Service at the Sky Harbor Airport returned the damaged Century training plane 2202 Zulu to flying status the morning of Ruth's projected cross–country flight.

Saturday morning dawned bright and clear over the metropolitan area of nearby New York. John, as usual, began flying at 9:00 A.M. It was a beautiful day, he pondered to himself. Virtually little wind and clear skies. An ideal day not only for students to fly solo but an excellent day for distant flying with no agitation from the elements. It was also the last day of the month. He was scheduled to start his new position with Amalgamated Pharmaceuticals Corporation on Monday.

Ruth was scheduled to fly at 2:00 P.M. with John, and this would be his last trip of the day. He had been wrestling with his problem of whether to resume his broken marriage for the sake of his children or marry Ruth. Since the previous Monday he had laid awake nights trying to rationalize with the problem. It was entirely a problem of conscience. Up to now, he had not as yet resolved it in his mind. He needed to be guided in the ultimate direction.

He flew a series of students almost every hour until 2:00 P.M. and then was ready to take Ruth for her first big trip. He looked forward all day long to this. She had become his one bright spot in life. Just to be alongside her was the grandest pleasure for him. When he came back into the flight Office at 2:00 P.M., she was waiting for him. She had a couple of new air navigation charts, a plastic flight plotter, and her undying enthusiasm. Her charts were air maps with prominent landmarks upon them.

She was wearing a short cotton dress, a button–up the front sweater, a pair of white open–toed shoes, and her brunette hair was gathered into an upsweep. She looked so freshly scrubbed as to be right out of a milk bath. Her face had a warm glow about it. There was no doubt that he loved this girl and would never get over her if he did force himself to give her up.

Together, at her home, they previously had plotted this course and a quick review was now made. They would be flying down to old Bader Airport in Atlantic City, New Jersey. They headed toward the rebuilt airplane 2202 Zulu. John inquired of the chief mechanic the condition of this newly rebuilt plane.

"Warren, is this plane going to hold up for us?"

"John, we rebuilt the whole front end of the basic frame, one wing, and it has a brand new propeller on it," he answered.

"What about the engine shaft?" John pressed him. "This plane damaged the propeller on the hard runway with the engine going. A shock like that with a turning metal propeller against a hard, paved runway can damage the shaft, I've been told."

"We magna–fluxed the shaft and miked the bearings. She's in fine shape. She runs up on test to perfection."

"Okay," said John. "We'll take it easy on her anyway."

The Century trainer was a two seat, side by side, high wing plane ideal for instruction purposes. It had a 100 H.P. engine of four cylinders. It had a cabin within its fuselage (Body) enclosed all around with a plexiglass windshield, giving it very good visibility. The front part of the cabin was open space from the forward instrument panel to a bulkhead more than six feet back into the fuselage.

Just back from the instrument panel were the two compact seats placed side by side. Behind the seats was a large baggage area capable of carrying 100 pounds of additional gross weight. The whole floor of the plane was covered with blue carpeting.

Ruth gave the plane a minute inspection and checked the full fuel tanks and oil tank. Both were filled to the brim. John had a temporary, queasy thought built on intuition about the plane but after a quick check of the propeller, he was satisfied.

Both he and Ruth took their respective seats aboard the tiny plane and taxied out to the end of Runway 9. A high overcast had started to gather, and it was apparent that the weather for the following day, Sunday, would not be good. As yet, though, the ceiling was high and the visibility was still ten miles.

Ruth ran up the engine and made a complete cockpit and control check and set her directional gyro (compass). Then she entered the runway for a takeoff toward the east. At full power, she broke ground, climbing out and around the airport to a height of 2,000 feet above sea level. Then she headed out on a course of almost due south to Atlantic City. The trip down would take somewhat better than an hour's time.

Ruth sat there in the left, or pilot's seat, as John sat in the right, or instructor's, seat. She checked her course on the map with its landmarks below. There was practically no wind correction to be made. The air was glass smooth. They skirted the Newark area and soon crossed the Raritan River.

John sat there with her beautiful body next to his. Her perfume, bath soap, and female pulchritude made him fully conscious of her presence. A slight glance at her legs, and he was aware of just one of her many charms. She had the prettiest legs he had ever viewed.

Occasionally he would ask her where they were to test her. She would point to a spot along the map and repeat regularly: "Right there, John." They had a private bet. If she found her destination, he had to buy the lunch. If she lost and needed help, she would have to pay for their lunch. The plane poked along at an airspeed of 95 M.P.H.

In a little while, they reached a point between Lakehurst Naval Air Station out on their right wing and Seaside Heights, the Jersey shore, out on their left wing. From then on they flew over pine tree country and washed out lowlands. Then the course left the mainland and traversed Barnegat Bay and Little Egg Harbor. Out on the crest of the Atlantic Ocean was a long sand bar upon which stood Atlantic City in all its splendor. Ahead of them about five miles, Ruth spotted the tall buildings and hotels of the great resort.

"There it is, John. I'll find the field in a few minutes. Get your lunch money ready. I just might decide to eat steak since you are going to pay for it," she laughed. She then picked up the microphone and dialed the standard Unicom frequency.

"Bader Unicom, Century 2202 Zulu, what is your active runway?"

Shortly came the reply. "Bader Unicom to Century 2202 Zulu, we are landing on Runway Niner."

Ruth had climbed to 2,000 feet enroute and now as the confines of Atlantic City were one mile away, she began cutting back on the power throttle, allowing the plane to progressively settle down to a lower altitude. Ahead of them, about two miles further south and just in off the ocean, she spotted the airport. It sure was in a convenient spot, she thought. A couple blocks from the Boardwalk.

John watched her with a wary eye but she knew just what to do. He had drilled into her every precaution. She came down to 1,000 feet and circled the airport in a left–hand traffic pattern. On the eastern fringe of the field, she passed over the famous Boardwalk, hotels, gambling casinos, and convention hall.

Another plane preceded her in on Runway 9. Then she lined up on the approach and let down. With the squeal of her tires and a slight bump, Ruth rolled out slowly. They turned onto the taxi strip and were shortly on the tiedown ramp.

"I'll have that lunch on you now, John. Did I take good care of you?"

"You did fine, Ruth. Nice trip. You're pretty good for a female pilot."

"We women are going to take over this world, John," she giggled.

"Oh boy. I think I'll move to another planet while I am able to," he joshed her.

They strode over to the flight office and registered. They then headed out the door to a nearby restaurant. They both ordered hot sandwiches and washed them down with thick milkshakes. At 4:00 P.M., they left the small restaurant and headed back to the nearby Bader Airport. It would be imperative to get moving northward.

They bid the manager of Bader Airport a so long and took their respective seats once more in the Century trainer. Ruth taxied out to Runway 9 and again checked out the engine and its instruments. All seemed okay.

She opened the throttle and in moments broke ground and climbed eastward over the hotels, and then proceeded northward along the boardwalk at 500 feet. John allowed her to stay at 500 feet in altitude, to see what she wanted to along the great promenade. Past the lighthouse, she turned northward and began climbing lazily on the homebound course.

Once more she pushed the throttle full on and sought to climb a bit higher. Below them were many desolate islands, inland sand bars, duck sanctuaries, and varied swampland. A couple of miles from Atlantic City, she leveled off to peer ahead.

The visibility had shrunk to four miles now and haze was moving in. Off to the west, the sun was declining into a murky overcast. There was still sufficient daylight to reach home base but it was increasingly apparent that bad weather was building up for the next day.

They heard a loud sudden bang and then the muffled noise of an engine rattling. The plane lost forward speed and traction. Hot oil sprayed the windshield. John jumped into action. The propeller shaft disintegrated. The propeller flew away. He cut back on the engine as the noise indicated the engine was running wild without its propeller. Since the engine would no longer avail him any power, he shut off the ignition switch. As the engine died in submission, he glanced below him.

Only the islands, sand bars, and swamp grass seemed available for a landing. He picked out the bigger of the islands and glided down, maintaining his air speed with the lowering of his nose. From above it seemed like a flat brown spot but as he neared its surface, he realized it was covered with brush and young bushes. He would have to land onto brush and cane.

At 300 feet he yelled at Ruth to tighten her safety belt and take the cushion behind her and put it in front of her face for protection. He lowered the flaps and stalled out in his flying speed. Five feet above the brush, he yanked back tightly on the control wheel, and the plane mushed into small brush and reeds, ending up on its nose.

CHAPTER | FOURTEEN

"Ruth, are you all right?"

"Yes, I'm okay. A slight bump on my knee but I'm all right."

"Okay, stay where you are for a minute until I get down out of here."

The aircraft stood up on its nose. Both of them sat facing forward at a sixty degree angle to level. They were hung up by their safety belts. John unbuckled his belt easily, pressing his feet forward against the rudder pedals so as not to fall further down.

He opened his side door easily but some of the wooden brush blocked him from opening the door wider. He forced it wide enough to squeeze down out of the doorway and then made his way around to Ruth's side of the aircraft. He broke off a few limbs of the low trees and then opened Ruth's door.

"Press your feet against the rudder pedals and then loosen your belt," he directed her. Quickly she followed his advice and let herself down from the inclined position. Once upon the ground, they both stood bewildered looking at the crippled plane. Actually, only the engine was destroyed. The metal propeller had liberated itself to God knows where—possibly the water.

He instinctively glanced at his watch and noted the time at 4:45 P.M. Only another forty–five minutes of daylight and then darkness. The only way off this island now would be by boat and there were none around.

"What happens now, John?"

"Well, for one thing, you are going to miss your date with Merle tonight. The next prospect is we will be stranded here tonight."

"Oh, tragic, tragic," Ruth lamented in mirth. "No date with Merle. How will I survive that one? And here alone with you. Oh! Oh!"

"Let's look about the island and see if we can spot any boats nearby. Maybe someone saw us come down," he suggested.

They were about one hundred feet in from the sandy shoreline bordering the bay that surrounded them. She held onto his arm as they walked the circumference of the almost semi–round, isolated sand bar. All over the island were small trees and brush. Many leaves had fallen off the trees in the late autumnal change. Here and there were small sunken marshes and tiny creeks reaching out to the bay.

John made a mental note that many of the trees were wild berry bushes and others were tiny pine trees. None of these trees were tall as both wind and high tides kept them at a low height. There were also large migrations of ducks. It was getting dark and there was no other sound other than the quacking of the ducks and fish skipping the water. Off in the distance were similar islands and swampland but no sign of another human being nearby.

At dusk they returned to the plane. He climbed upon the fuselage to the tail of the plane and his body weight caused it to settle down to a near level position.

The front edges of the wings were slightly scuffed but, all in all, the plane itself didn't seem too bad off. It might still fly another day. As the fuselage settled back upon the brush, its tail canted upward at an angle of 10 degrees. About them on the sandy loam were both land and sea crabs. Ruth was edgy with her open–toed shoes, fearing one might bite her foot.

Dampness was in the air and visibility was shrinking fast. The next day's weather was definitely going to be rainy. Ruth tightened her sweater about her and John still had his leather flight jacket on. She was still shivering at this beginning of November temperatures. He decided to build a fire out of the dry limbs and tall tan reeds about him. He set up a small fireplace with a circle of stones, just in under the left wing panel as there was less brush on that side.

He drained a pinch of gasoline from the quick–drain under the high wing panel and squirted it on a few of the broken reeds he had gathered. Since neither one of them was a smoker, they had no matches. He disconnected a wire from a spark plug on the engine. Then he got Ruth to turn on the ignition with the key. The spark plug fired up a piece of the gas soaked reeds and with this, he got a fire going.

He then got Ruth to try to raise someone in the air by the radio UNICOM set. But either there was no one in the vicinity or perhaps the antenna had been damaged. Almost dark now and in the glare of the fire, he got out a little tool kit that was carried in the glove compartment and began moving the two individual seats from the cabin.

As darkness finally closed in about them, both of them huddled under the left wing and around the fire. Ruth sat upon the pilot seat placed just outside her door of the fuselage while John placed his seat on the opposite side of the small fire. Periodically, he would get up and, within the glare of the fire, gather more broken wood and tan swamp reeds for fuel. He now had brought in and stockpiled about eight armloads of wood, sufficient for the night.

"What do you think will happen now, John?"

"They won't miss us till dark at Sky Harbor. After that they will be waiting for a phone call. After that or, by tomorrow, well...."

"Think we will be found by tomorrow?" she queried.

"All I can say with truth is that its a good thing we ate before we left Bader Airport. By tomorrow they will start a hunt for us."

"John, if I'm to be lost for a day or two, I'm awfully glad it is with you. It's romantic," she said then smiled at him with that devilishly warm grin of hers.

"We will be found possibly by tomorrow noon. No doubt about it. Just don't catch cold in the meantime," he cautioned her.

Ruth kept her feet up off the ground so the occasional land crab crawling about would not bite her through her open–toed shoes. John got a laugh out of it. She put her feet up on the left wheel of the landing gear and nestled down into her seat.

"Ruth, it's going to rain sometime tonight. We will have to sleep in the cabin on the floor. There's enough room in there to stretch out. I'll wait out here till it starts and then I might have to get in there with you. Any objections?"

"Well, well, alone on a deserted island with my favorite man. I wonder what Merle will say to that? Whhheeee!"

"You little devil. We are in a serious jam and all you can think of is romance. I hope Merle finds us tonight and carries you home," he teased her and laughed.

She stuck her tongue out at him. After more trivial talk, she became drowsy and he told her to crawl into the cabin but to leave the door open so the heat of the fire might reach her.

He sat alone with his thoughts. It had been miraculous that neither one of them was hurt. He would have to make some provision tomorrow for food. It might be some time before they were found. He fell asleep in the seat and drowsed away.

Sometime in the early morning he awoke with the rain beating against him. The fire was just smoldering ashes. He set to work rebuilding it. The rain blew in under the wing soaking the wet branches he put upon it. Then the heat of the fire took hold and flared into life again.

He then took his place in Ruth's seat near the door which was under the widest part of the wing. The rain blew in from the eastern side of the fuselage whereas, the fuselage pointed to the north. His chances of getting wet now were less. Only the breeze would occasionally carry the rain to him.

The fuselage was a barricade against the windward side. Near dawn Ruth woke up and pleaded with him to get into the plane while she tended the fire.

He was tired by now and didn't need much coaxing. As Ruth got out of the cabin, with her wrinkled dress, John sprawled on the floor of the cabin for a few winks.

When he awoke two hours later, Ruth had a good fire going, and the two of them gathered together around it. He then went out about fifty feet away from the plane in the downpour and built a bivouac–type latrine over to the right side of the plane and out of view from the left side of the fuselage. Then he showed it to her.

"Where did you get the idea for this latrine, John?"

"I used to be a Boy Scout when I was a youngster and then, of course, the Air Force taught us a course in survival tactics." He had built a series of tough branches together to form a seat and back rest over a small clear spot.

By laying two identical branches a foot apart and parallel, both of which rested on the Y–shaped trunks of short trees, plus a higher one for a back rest, it would serve its purpose.

"Use a few of those leaves for your needs," he laughed.

After both of them dried the raindrops off their clothes and bodies around the fire, he removed the two aluminum wingtips from the ends of the wings. These were deep, concave pieces that were attached by metal screws to the wingtips for streamline purposes. He stuck both of these over the fire to sterilize them. After awhile, he removed them and placed them atop the wings to catch rain water.

"The bay water is too salty and fishy to drink. But we will now gather pure drinking water."

CHAPTER | FIFTEEN

John removed the two aluminum tips on the ends of the stabilizer, which was the short wing on the tail assembly. After sterilizing these, he told Ruth to mind the store while he went looking for berries.

"Not without me, John."

"Okay, come along," he smiled.

They walked in the cold drizzle around the island and collected a container of berries. Some were nearly dried out but still juicy. They would provide nourishment for them. Then John spied a mess of ducks drifting offshore. He gathered several rocks and after five throws, managed to kill one duck.

A couple of hours later they returned to the plane drenched to the skin. He took down one of the aluminum tips off the wing. It now had an inch of water within it.

"Here, Ruth. Take a swig of this before you dehydrate."

He placed the tip back up on the wing with its other mate to gather more rain water. Ruth set to work trying to rig up a broiler for the dead duck while John plucked the feathers from it and cleaned out its insides. He then took a cable off the engine and ran it through the duck. Ruth suspended the cable with its speared duck across the fire and watched it slowly turn brown and broil.

"Wait here, Ruth. I'm going to try for more of those ducks. You won't be afraid, will you?"

"I'm getting braver by the minute, but don't be long," she pleaded.

He was gone an hour now and she called out loud to him. He heard her from the opposite side of the island and presently returned with two more beaned ducks. If they were going to be here for awhile, they were not going to go hungry.

"Dinner is ready. Come and get it while its hot," she laughed.

He walked into the bay on the sandy beach and washed his hands. Then Ruth followed and washed her hands in the bay water. Both of them were beginning to look dirty and rather decrepit by now but didn't seem to notice it. The rain came down in torrents. He made no attempt to call over the radio, preferring to save the plane's battery until a more clearer day.

In between errands, he managed to dry out by the fire. When they finally sat down to eat, it was with a tremendous appetite.

"You can't say that I'm not taking you to the best restaurants, Ruth."

"And you can't say I'm not a good cook either," she retorted. "All you need is a napkin."

"Are you going to wash the dishes now?" he chided her. "Just don't use too much soap."

"I won't wash them if you don't dry them," she shot back at him.

Back at Sky Harbor, no information on John and Ruth's whereabouts were known. A long distance call to Bader Airport on Sunday morning elicited the information they had arrived there safely and left for homebase at approximately 4:00 P.M. Then they disappeared.

"If they are down and no telephone call, they might be in the ocean," suggested one pessimist.

"They must be down in the pine country," another party suggested.

"It could be they may be laying injured in some remote area," another suggested.

The newspapers, radio, and particularly the television newscast, got wind of the disappearance and by Sunday night the country was alerted that Pilot John Maloney, a flight instructor, had been lost with a woman student, Ruth Reynolds. They also reported that she was employed at the same flying service and had known each other for some time. No mention was made at the time of the possibility of equipment failure.

The immediate effect on those at home was strenuous. Ruth's mother was beside herself with the worry of her daughter's safety. She was bolstered by her other grown children.

Martha heard the news, and when she introduced herself as John's wife, she gave a conflicting story to the media that perhaps he had eloped with this Ruth Reynolds. This set off a series of rumors that mushroomed. It made for nasty gossip. It put Martha in the role of a silent suffering martyr with two babies for whom to care.

"I kept after him for years to give up this damn flying business. But he refused to listen. I remain here at home with my two little daughters."

Most of the resources of the aviation industry, state police, and all communities were given notice to start searching for them. Those back at Sky Harbor knew they had inadvertently been forced down somewhere along their trail homeward. The civil air patrol was given the job of air search. But they would all have to wait on the weather.

By late Sunday afternoon, John had piled up a vast stack of firewood and seasoned brown reeds. He had killed four ducks, plucked them, and gathered a reservoir of fresh drinking rain water from the rain swollen skies. The rain let up slightly only to be replaced by heavy fog and mists.

"Come on, Ruth. Let's take a walk around while the rain has let up and gather more berries for our breakfast tomorrow."

They hiked about the island hand in hand for about an hour. At one point Ruth lost her shoe and John had to retrieve it for her. At another point, he had to carry her over a creek. Toward dusk they strode back toward the plane, arm in arm and wet with moisture. The fire, now smoldering, needed rejuvenation. Another bundle of wood brought it back to life. They then sat almost atop the fire trying to get warmer.

The smell of food cooking brought a hoard of sand flies to the vicinity of the plane, and the damp air made them cling to the skin. They kept the windows and doors of the plane closed to keep them outside. The smoke and heat of the fire kept them at a distance. Ruth was no longer timid about the land crabs and by now she wasn't afraid to kick them out of her way.

They washed up in the bay water and then sat about the fire talking. John told Ruth his capsuled life story and Ruth told of her short life span.

"When I was stationed in California, we had a rainy season of three days just like this. I remember once we had to wait on the weather. In the Gulf War, we had a severe sand storm that kept us on the ground from taking off."

"I was a majorette for our high school football team," Ruth told him. "All the men used to stare at my short skirt and legs and whistle. It made me feel so self–conscious."

"I like looking at your beautiful legs myself, Ruth," he teased her.

"You had better not ever stop looking at my legs, John. After we get off this island, I'm afraid people are going to talk."

"Let's turn in, Ruth."

He put a few more sticks on the fire and then he and Ruth got in on the floor of the plane. The width of the fuselage tapered slightly narrower as it bent toward the tail. The narrow part permitted both of them to lay down side by side with about the width of a cot. Ruth used her purse as a small head cushion and she threw her sweater and his leather jacket across the both of them.

It started raining hard and the raindrops pounded against the aluminum siding and heavily upon the outstretched wings. Ruth was breathing hard, and John lay there fully conscious of her body pressed sideways to his. So much so, that he stirred up on one elbow and whispered to her.

"Ruth, I love you."

She turned toward him now and slowly replied: "I love you too, John."

He reached for her, gathering her into his arms and kissing her on the mouth and all about her cheeks, neck, and shoulders. His hands sought her breasts. She did not repulse him. She closed her eyes as her arms went around his neck. They were both in heat. He now sought her completely. His head bent as he opened her dress and fondled and kissed her well rounded breasts. She was completely aroused.

His hands reached for her legs, caressing her knees and smooth thighs and his hands took complete charge of her intimate region. "I need you, Ruth. I need you."

Her hands drew him tightly to her. In the darkness of the cabin, he made intimate contact with her. His deep, labored breathing and her ecstatic sighing and moaning with fiery passion gave out a strong hint of the warmth that passed between them. After time had passed and both were exhausted, he dropped down beside her. Grasping her hand in his, he fell asleep.

The heavy rain continued its rhythmic beat upon the metallic structure of the plane, reminding one that the inside cabin was a warm, comfortable refuge in which to be isolated. What had now transpired between them was but the beginning of a dynamic relationship that was destined to last all the rest of their dual lives.

In spite of these dismal surroundings; the very humble inconveniences; the raw conditions of this sudden, awkward adventure, they had descended down inadvertently to this seemingly great paradise of togetherness.

CHAPTER | SIXTEEN

Ruth stirred from her uncomfortable position on the carpeted metal floor of the plane. The early morning rain was still tapping the wings above her. In the gray, murky dawn, she reached for John subconsciously, and he was not there. She looked above her at the low ceiling of the cabin gathering her thoughts. It was cold, and her dress did not reach far down enough to cover her legs.

Suddenly sensing her loneliness, she sprang up and just as quickly relaxed. John was out under the left wing trying to revive the fire. He took another stick and held it under one of the quick–drains to dampen it with gasoline. He then opened the cowling of the engine and held a loose but wire–secured spark plug to the gas–soaked limb. Seeing Ruth sitting upright now, he told her to turn on the ignition and fire up the engine.

In a few moments, the limb he was holding was enflamed from the spark that emitted. He then used it to get the fire going and began getting the pan of berries for their ersatz breakfast.

"Hi, Honey. Did you sleep well?"

"Fairly well but I feel so stiff all over. Still raining, hey?"

"Thank you for last night, Ruth. I love you, Honey." He touched her shoulder with his hand and then kissed her.

"I shouldn't have let you, John. But down here like this, somehow it seemed so right."

"That was your first time, wasn't it Ruth?" he grinned.

"Now how in blazes would you know? What makes you think you know everything?"

"I could tell, Ruth. I'll keep your secret forever."

"I was saving my favors for the right man when he married me. Now here I am, a fallen woman."

The two of them sat about downing berries and drinking rain water that had filled up the wingtip containers. It was very cold in the early morning dampness as the first week of November was beginning on this dismal Monday morning.

"Looks like it is going to rain forever," she said as she munched several handfuls of berries.

"Ruth, we may be stuck here for some time. It may mean we will have to live a very primitive existence. Can you take it?" he asked.

"If it doesn't bother you, it shouldn't bother me," she replied emphatically.

"You know that I gave notice of quitting Zenith as of yesterday. Today, I was supposed to report for instructions with Amalgamated. I might wind up unemployed.

"I don't want to kill that battery prematurely, but while I'm gathering some more wood and dead reeds, try and contact someone of the emergency frequency. Try it for half an hour and then shut it off." He then went foraging around in the light drizzle for more wood and an occasional look for a boat or two out on the rain spattered bay.

Since the temperature seemed to be getting lower each morning, he felt the necessity of piling up great amounts of wood from the dead trees and berry bushes. He gathered enough for the next three days. Ruth patiently strived to raise someone with her radio calls but the radio set would not communicate from ground to ground and the weather prevented her from talking to another plane under such foggy conditions.

"Ruth, I'm going after more ducks. Will you cook two of these?"

"Okay, John," she answered and resumed singing a light song she was muddling through. He marveled at her composure.

He had brought in four ducks the day before, of which they had eaten one between them. Now Ruth prepared to cook two more of them, leaving one in reserve. She remained under the wing of the plane near the fire.

She walked out to the tip of the wing and severed the neck and feet from each duck with her sharpened nail file from her purse. She plucked all the feathers from them as she had watched John do the day before. She strung them on the steel flexible cable that John had taken off the engine.

John was now gone two hours and finally came back with three more dead ducks beaned with rocks. He hung these up in a nearby tree, making four more ducks in reserve. He sat down by the fire and dried off. Ruth poured some rain water over the ducks, trying to brown them and keep moisture in them.

He watched her as she puttered about. She sure was taking everything in stride. It was a good thing too because it was beginning to look as though they might be here for several more days.

"Ruth, did you enjoy last night?" She sat there with both of her legs together and her short dress tucked tightly under her thighs. As she sat there, her feet kept vibrating up and down on her toes as though she was getting ready to dance. She smiled with a blush at the question and put her head down. Then she sneaked a look at him and caught him laughing at her.

About noontime she removed the ducks from the fire and each one grabbed a duck and started filling their ravenous appetites with the delicious white meat. Once again the flies and gnats gathered about them but did not come too close because of the fire. As a land crab would approach her, she would gently lift it up with her open–toed shoe and send it flying off a dozen feet away from her.

After they finished the noonday meal of roast duck, berries and rain water, the two of them strolled into the bay and washed their hands and face.

"Oh what I would give for a cake of soap right now and a toothbrush," she drooled.

"I'm getting mixed up as to what day it is," said John.

After they dried off by the fire, there seemed to be nothing further for them to do but sit and talk. The rain picked up in intensity. Ruth sat there with her legs propped up on the left landing wheel and John could hold out no longer. It was 2:00 p.m. in the afternoon. He threw a few more pieces of wood on the fire, then walked over to Ruth.

"Ready for lesson number two?"

"What does that consist of?"

"We will now proceed with more patience and confidence and practice our lessons," he laughed.

He opened the door of the cabin plane and took her hand into the fuselage. He shut the door of the plane. The heat of the fire reflected against the side of the fuselage. He laid her down on the blue carpeted metal floor and then embraced her. He kissed her mouth, her neck, her shoulders, and then drew her full round breasts out, burying his face into them.

Her blue eyes lighted up with fire, and she started panting for breath. His hands went all around her waist touching her hips, her chest, and caressed her arms. He kissed her all over her neck and then his hands sought her full thighs. He was now in terrific heat. His hands ran wild over her frame.

She was fully aroused and then his hands removed her panties exposing most of her beautiful, artistic body. He pushed her hemline up to her waist and then as the rain beat down overhead on the wings, he made contact with her.

Her eyes opened and closed. She momentarily tried to push him away but it was no use. He mastered her with his powerful but gentle way. Time was allowed to lapse as they adjusted to each other. A few whispered words of encouragement, a sigh, an ecstatic moan and erotic movements of first his and then both of their bodies in unison—a rhythm as old as time itself.

Without separating, they had a mutual orgasm and remained intact as his hands renewed his zest for her by caressing her lovely body again and again. Then finally exhausted, both of them fell asleep side by side. It was near darkness when they both awoke and were again hungry and thirsty.

Ruth got up and out first, stepping out the cabin door with her things. As John got up she was nowhere near. He went looking for her and there she was at the beach, stark naked trying to bathe herself without soap. Then she wrung her dress and underwear out.

"I thought you were afraid of going in there, Ruth?"

"I was but I feel so in need of a bath, I'm willing to risk it," she smiled at him. Then he removed his clothes and plunged into the cold water after her. He splashed water at her as she screamed at him. After both had refreshed themselves in the bitter cold bay water, he gave her the clothes to hold, then he picked her up and carried her back to the plane.

Both of them sat about the fire trying to get warm and hanging their clothes on the strut holding up the wing that was in under the wing. All about them was fog, haze, and heavy clouds of moisture. The red flame of the fire cast weird red shadows dancing upon their bodies as they waited for their clothes to dry.

Ruth had lost all her bobby pins, and her once carefully cultivated hair that had been in an upsweep was now in disarray about her shoulders. John eyed her up. *She is beautiful*, he thought to himself, and so dependent upon him now.

"You look like a prehistoric caveman with that growing beard, John."

"You look like my Polynesian beauty," he murmured.

They sat there talking back and forth till almost midnight. Their clothes finally dried and warm but wrinkled. They donned them in preparation for the long night's sleep ahead of them. Then they turned in and curled up in each other's arms. They clung so tightly to one another that coldness could not penetrate their bodies.

Back home in the meantime, the newspapers and television played up the story that perhaps as the poor, distraught, and long–suffering Martha had suggested, John and Ruth may have eloped. It made for hot copy.

It was a very derogative story but Ruth's mother rose to defend her daughter by saying that Ruth would never elope without telling her about it. Also Mrs. Reynolds pressed the reporters to tell the real story, that John had been divorced by Martha over a year ago. She said Martha's side of the story was dramatic quackery designed to create questionable sympathy for herself. Then the media checked out the facts and changed the whole concept of the story.

Mr. Herlihy of Amalgamated Pharmaceutical Corporation advised the media that he had promised John employment as a pilot with his corporation. He would remain adamant. He would hold to his promised position to John Maloney until they were found.

The Zenith Flying Service had only good things to say of Pilot John Maloney and his fine, careful, piloting skills. He had safely flown for them for over six years.

All attempts at trying to find them would still have to wait on the weather.

CHAPTER | SEVENTEEN

Ruth stirred at dawn. She was laying sideways facing John and her left leg lay across him. Her skirt was surprisingly up to her waist, exposing her pink panties. John was sleeping soundly. Slightly embarrassed she removed her leg and struggled to pull her dress down closer to her knees.

She turned away from him to the opposite side, and her back was to him. He half awoke at that moment and snuggled closer to her. His arm went across her right shoulder with his hand trying to cover her. Her sweater and his leather jacket was all the cover they had.

He pressed closer to her trying to keep her from freezing. She then felt warmer with his warm body on her back. There seemed no hurry to getting up. It was just going to be another rainy day.

Ruth lay there wondering what manner of fate had struck her down into this lonesome island with this man whom she loved. At that moment, she would not have wanted it any other way. She had found grand happiness being here with him. He was so gentle, so protective, and so warm. But what does he really think of her now that she had given herself to him? Would he respect her when they finally left this forsaken island?

He had not as yet proposed to her. He had only declared his love for her and she for him. But once leaving this island, what might she expect from him? How terrible it would be to lose him. She whimpered at the thought. Why did there have to be that double standard that made a woman so dependent upon a man's whims? Would he still return to his former wife for the sake of his children?

She started to shake and cry. He woke up and then asked if she was dreaming.

"What is the matter, Honey?"

"John, do you truly love me as you say you do?"

He turned her around to him. His left arm went under her neck as he cradled her close to him. Her head lay now on his shoulder. He reached for the curve of her buttocks and pulled her left leg up and across his waist.

"Now just what is the matter, Ruth? What is it that is bugging you?"

"John, will you respect me now that I have given you what you want?"

"You have not given me everything I want, Ruth. In fact, its going to take you at least fifty years to give me everything I want from you. I love you that much. I'll never stop loving you. But I must still settle something back home as yet. Can you wait for me?"

"You are seeing me at my worst, John."

His black beard was out thick on his face now. It was Tuesday morning and he had not shaved since Saturday morning. The rain had apparently stopped temporarily for everything was quiet in the eerie stillness. The only noise outside was the sudden winging of an occasional bird or the quacking of ducks. It was so still that Ruth clung even tighter to him for that feeling of security that makes women tremble at times.

"I think my mother must be beside herself with worry about me at this moment. I haven't been home with her in four days. She is probably calling Zenith every couple of hours for some hopeful information about us. I sure hope my brother and sister are near to comfort her. If only we had some way of letting her know we are all right."

"I missed visiting my daughters yesterday. They, too, must be filled with apprehension."

He got up then went outside to restart the smoldering ashes of the fire. He would use the same familiar pattern he had done the last several days. Then he went looking for more berries, returning in an hour to where she nervously awaited him. She took down two more dead ducks and prepared them for roasting as she had done the previous day.

He went out again now, hunting ducks. He returned with four of them, and by that time, Ruth had a noontime feast spread for him. She also used some water in the aluminum wingtip and dipped in the berries to put moisture in them. It was so late in the season that the berries had long since passed their peak in taste.

There was no wind and no rain, just a perpetual fog hanging about the area. They could see about five–hundred feet ahead of them. After their noontime meal, Ruth set about putting two more ducks over the fire. Then she and John took a walk all around the island arm in arm, for want of exercise and more berries. She was bubbling over with happiness at the amount of time and attention he showered on her.

In exchange John could not help but be attentive toward her. She had so many cute ways and humorous expressions that she had completely captivated him. She certainly was *Miss Personality Plus*. They were devoted to each other as though no other person existed in the world. They were the only two people alive at that moment. It was almost as though both of them secretly hoped that they might never be found.

At the far end of the island, he stopped and took Ruth into his arms. He crushed her while they stood facing each other.

"Ruth, you are beautiful. Don't ever leave me for another," he pleaded.

"Gee, John. What do you see in me now? Up until last week I used to try to look so pretty for you. My hair would be so neat. My perfume the best, the seam in my stockings so perfectly straight, deodorant and soap under my armpits, and now, here I am looking terrible and you profess your love for me."

"Did you really try that hard to catch my eye? Well, I'm in the same predicament. No soap, no razor, no change of clothing. I'll bet I look like a bum."

"If only I could wear my teddy bear pajamas when I turn in with you," she laughed.

"Forget the pajamas. I'd love to see you in a very lacy nightgown and lace pink panties."

"No pajamas. Why not pajamas?"

"Too masculine," he retorted. "I used to think you were just a sweet kid. Now I see you as a beautiful, lovely woman ready for a long life of love, love, and more love."

"Look at my dress and slip. They are so dirty now and my underwear, uuhhhh."

"As long as they are pink, it suits me fine," he laughed.

He again took her into his arms and crushed her to him. For several moments, he could not let go of her. Her blue eyes closed as she felt the pangs of passion running through her veins. Whatever it was that brought her down here to this remote spot with him, it certainly solved an adjustment problem in a hurry.

Leisurely they returned to the plane, cold, damp, and in need of warmth. They had more ducks, more berries, and a thirst for drinking water. With their watches set for Standard Time, it was late in the afternoon when they returned. Ruth would start supper again and both of them went into the inlet beach they used for washing.

The path to the beach was well worn now and the slithering of land crabs and an occasional turtle no longer fazed Ruth. Also the path to the crude latrine was no longer a problem to her.

John had fashioned a long walking stick for her to brush aside the branches here and thee. He had also piled up a load of leaves in place of paper.

"Those leaves are a bit rough on my posterior, John."

"I told you we would be living primitive, Honey. I never promised you a rose garden."

Fortunately for both of them, they did not catch cold. The elements that endangered them seemed also to be conditioning them for the rigors of life. They had their evening meal of duck, berries, and drinking water in total darkness except for the light of the fire. Then they sat about talking.

CHAPTER | EIGHTEEN

"Turn on channel 7, Ruth. Bring on the dancing girls."

"If I had a cherry cordial right now, I just might give you that dancing girl for whom you are looking."

She sat there with her big warm smile on her face and her pretty knees looking fresh and dainty as though she were some Smoky Mountain gal sitting in a country store. His hand reached for her, and he stroked her knees and calves.

"When we get back to civilization, you are going to have to beg me for my favors," Ruth teased him. "I'll not be so generous with you then."

"Then I had better make up for lost time now," he laughed. Her eyes watched him, hoping he might take care of that volatile feeling that was rising in her. He had opened up that dam of passion within her and now her hot feelings and curiosity were running riot within her.

He threw more wood on the fire and then turned to her. "Let's turn in now, Honey. I need you."

They both turned in, and he began fondling her. As he drew her to him in the darkness lighted by the outside glare of the fire, it seemed to him that never before in his life had he been as excited as she seemed to make him. Her soft, warm, smooth curves were like magic to him. His hands ran all over her lower extremities as his mouth kissed all of her above the waist. They made contact.

She was so excited she could not talk, only gasp as he coached her through the world's oldest rhythm. They made love repeatedly for hours until finally both were drained of emotion, without a single nerve alive in their bodies.

Then they fell asleep holding hands in the tiny cabin with very little room for anything other than straight sleeping. One could not turn without the other knowing it. He was extremely gentle with her.

Knowing in his heart that it was himself who first penetrated her, he felt a strong responsibility toward her. He would wake up occasionally and cover her with her sweater or dovetail her legs in between his to keep her warm.

During the nights, the temperature would drop as low as 35 degrees Fahrenheit and go up to 48 degrees during the day. Winter was fast approaching. Wednesday and Thursday passed by without any change in the wet, soggy weather. It would rain occasionally in torrents and stop only to provide fog and low hanging mists about them. They were no longer sure of what day it was. Trying to keep warm was the important item.

"Will it ever stop raining, John?"

"It will have to, Ruth. Even the sky will need to refill its clouds. Only the sun can do that.

"Ruth, if you married a man and all he could afford was a four–room bungalow, would you still love him?"

"Right now I have been living with you a whole week in a tiny fuselage and you ask me a dumb, silly question like that. Just what is it that is bugging you, John?"

"Golly, that is right. I didn't look at it that way. It is just another question running through my mind. But suppose we had to stay here forever," he teased her.

"I'm beginning to think it might be a good idea to keep you here, John. That's why I chased those two fishing boats away last night while you slept. I told them you were my prisoner. So they left."

"You wouldn't dare," he laughed.

Friday morning was just like the previous mornings, a heavy rain pounding on the wings and fuselage above them but yet so cold and miserable. He lay facing her. Her back was toward him as he sought to keep her warm. She was like a little kitten to him, his arms both under her neck and around her shoulders, her legs doubled backward between his pant legs, her sweater covering the front of her.

It was the crampness of the quarters that finally induced them to stir into life. He got up first and once again sought to start the fire. Once more he soaked a stick of wood with gasoline drained from the wing tank. He tried to ignite it through the spark plug but now the battery was dead. This would be the last time they could use the battery for starting the fire.

Henceforth, he would have to use another method of starting the fire. He used an old Boy Scout trick of soaking two rocks with gasoline, piling a few dry leaves together, then banging the rocks together till they sparked and flared suddenly. It ignited the dried leaves but it was tough on his hands. Once again the fire warmed both of them up and Ruth prepared to cook two more ducks for a noontime meal.

All the berries were gone now and only the ducks and rain water would provide them with nourishment. John came back after foraging around, with just one more duck.

"I think the ducks are getting wise to us, Honey. They are telling one another to stay away from this island. Its a slaughterhouse. We better save these last two ducks for tomorrow. Then I guess I'll go fishing with your last bobby–pin."

The rain was cascading down in sheets now as the two of them huddled under the wing. The rain sought to drench the fire so John made a screen by using his shirt and her sweater dangling from the trailing edge of the wing. They foiled the wind driven rain by suspending these garments with the aid of rocks atop the wing.

"We are here six days now, the way I count," Ruth mentioned. "Think they will ever find us?"

"I think we are here seven days, Ruth, unless that amorous afternoon with you loused up my count."

"When I get you back to civilization, John, I'm going to beat you with a club and work you over real good."

"Gee, I'd better run now," he laughed.

Meanwhile, back at Sky Harbor, the gang still worried about them. It was the premier topic of conversation. This rainstorm continued grounding all flight activity. Not an aircraft had moved about the airport since a week ago. Even some of the airline traffic was grounded at times.

Marian spoke up now. "He was a grand guy, very handsome, and she always had a big crush on him. She never once said so. But I knew she did. Wherever they are, unless they are injured, they are together. I really believe that she is happy at this moment. Gee, I wish they could be found. I would welcome both of them with open arms and kisses. God help them."

"I keep thinking, Ruth, that maybe I'll make you pregnant."

"If you do, I won't tell you, John."

"Why not?"

"Because then you would feel obligated toward me. I don't ever want to trap a man. I want a man to marry me because he really wants me, not because he has to."

"I'd be entitled to know."

"Yes, but not until years later."

"You're a sweet, funny kid. It so happens that I love you regardless of your possible condition."

She eyed him now, trying to tell him how much he really meant to her and how, though marooned, she considered it a blessing just to be here alone with him. If only he could look into her heart at that moment.

They ate part of their ducks but decided to save much of it till later in the day. As they gnawed at the legs of the ducks, they extricated every tiny morsel of meat, not allowing any of it to be wasted. Although they had sufficient drinking water, John insisted in putting the extra aluminum tips he had used to collect berries that were now all gone to increase the gathering of rain water in them.

He pondered that they might hit a dry period over a protracted dry spell. There was still sufficient firewood about.

Both of them were totally "hippy" looking. He had not shaved in a week. His clothes were torn from the brambles of the branches. Filth from the many labors he had performed and soot from the fire had added to the disheveled look about him.

She was still beautiful in face and figure but her soft shoes were now broken. Her bright clothes of a week ago were now filthy without soap to wash them. Her long black hair hung straight down at her shoulders. She made a vain effort each day to dress it up with a comb from her purse but the constant rain would stymie her efforts.

It became increasingly apparent that the two of them would make a couple of skid row characters at that moment, but the amazing part in all of this was that neither one was downcast. Their inward confidence that they would be found as the weather improved beguiled them into surviving.

Each regarded the experience together as a silent, beautiful chapter in their lives. Their humor was boundless and their spirits harmonious. If it did not bother John, it did not bother Ruth was the way she took it all in stride. He had some dire misgivings at times but did not communicate them to her. Her complete security meant everything to him at that time. He knew in his heart he could never stop loving this wonderful, affectionate girl here beside him.

"When did you first start noticing me, John?"

"I noticed you the very first day you started working at the airport. I figured you were a real sweet kid," he told her.

"I fell for you until I heard you were married, then I backed off," she admitted to him.

"I liked your cute ways, Ruth. You also had such a cute face and those gorgeous legs made me look at you every day."

At about 1:00 P.M., the rain stopped, a breeze picked up, and then the ceiling seemed to rise up. All about them the mists and low scud clouds hung over the water of the bay. Then suddenly he noticed a little trace of blue sky peeking out through the partial high overcast. The wind changed to the west and began to pick up in velocity.

"Its starting to clear at last, Honey."

By 2:00 P.M., the sun started to brighten up the area, and they could now look out over the water for a mile or two. The sun was declining also, but the sight of the sunshine cheered them both. It had been almost a week of continuous rain and moisture.

The sudden noise of an aircraft broke the stillness. Then they caught sight of a helicopter to the west of them but it was headed south.

CHAPTER | NINETEEN

"Ruth, have you got a mirror in your purse?"

"Yes, here it is."

The helicopter was going south but about a half mile to the west of them. The noise of its loud cluttering of windmilling vanes drawing their attention. John caught the sun's rays on the mirror and tried to reflect them toward the chopper. The sparkle of the sun's rays did hit the cockpit of the chopper.

The pilot of the helicopter turned to his co-pilot beside him and said: "There is someone out there trying to draw our attention. Let's find out what it is."

Almost past them now, the helicopter suddenly turned and came toward them. John kept signaling toward it. The helicopter was up at about fifteen hundred feet.

It started circling them. Then it came lower. The two U.S. Naval pilots aboard had spotted them and circled the crashed aircraft. Again it circled, coming lower and lower. It was now at 500 feet above them and studying them.

"Wave your arms, Ruth. Quick. Let them see us here."

The pilot aboard the Naval helicopter could not effect a rescue or even a radio contact with them. But he quickly related his find of a crashed aircraft and obviously live passengers, to the U.S. Naval Air Base at Lakehurst, New Jersey. Naval authorities quickly alerted two of its large rescue helicopters. It also alerted the state police and the air safety inspectors of both the Federal Aeronautical Authority and the New Jersey Aviation Committee.

News of the finding of the lost flyers went out over the teletype to all wire services. In but half an hour after the Navy was alerted, two giant helicopters of its air-sea rescue service appeared on the scene. The original smaller helicopter remained on picket duty to guide the rescue units. One came down to within twenty feet of the ground. Out of its side door came a medical crewman on a cable.

Then down came a breeches buoy on a cable winch. The crewman held the buoy while John prepared to put Ruth aboard. The huge gale kicked up by the rotor blades of the chopper blew all about them, rocking the wrecked plane and their whole little camp.

Ruth looked all about her and started to cry. Somehow she did hate to leave all this just yet—maybe if they could have just one more day together before returning to reality.

"Why are you crying, Ruth. We're safe now?"

"You would not understand, John."

"Maybe I do at that. Come on, Ruth, up you go now."

He fastened her into the rescue seat, strapping her in. The winch drew her up above them. The cable reached the cabin where she was freed of it and secured into a seat.

Then the cable was lowered and John was put aboard and hoisted up to the cabin under the twirling blades of the helicopter. Finally the crewman arrived up with them. The helicopter with its two lost victims headed back toward the Lakehurst Naval Air Station.

The rescue was effected just before 4:30 P.M. At 5:00 P.M. darkness closed about the island that they later found to be nicknamed Mystic Island on the geology charts.

Naval authorities met the rescue helicopter with cots and ambulances. They were rushed to the Naval Hospital where they were immediately checked by doctors for ill effects. Both of them were separated for the first time, and Ruth was taken to a female section used by nurses and female personnel. She was given fresh female uniform clothing.

Asked what she most wanted, she replied: "Please, let me into a shower for at least a half hour and let me have plenty of soap."

Civilian as well as Naval photographers took them through the various phases of their rehabilitation. John also got a hot shower and fresh clothing. Further medical checks, needles for shots against disease, and then both of them were reunited at the commander's table for a big supper.

After they both were fed, they were gathered in the main office of the Naval Commander of the base where civilian as well as Naval reporters heard them relate the facts of the crash. Both were allowed to make telephone calls, and Ruth was surprised when her mother related that she had just heard the happy news over the television. They were ordered to bed for the night.

"How soon may we go home, sir?"

"Perhaps tomorrow if our physicians find you both in good health. How do you both feel?"

John called Zenith Flying Service at Sky Harbor. They promised to fly down and pick them up with one of their planes if permission to land could be obtained.

The next day, the newspapers headlined the rescue with glaring headlines. "Lost Flyers Found." Then all the details in the lesser print.

"Lost propeller and broken crankshaft forced them to crash land on a tiny, uninhabited island. They survived on ducks, berries, and rain water. Naval Authorities had found and rescued them."

That was the substance of the heavy, dramatic, and emotional news copy. They woke up Saturday morning and were fed, then were again checked by the naval physicians. Both of them were dressed in Naval fatigue clothes. John just had his wallet and car keys. The rest of his clothes had to be burned. Ruth now wore Navy Wave fatigue clothes with just her purse as original equipment. Both of their cars were back at Sky Harbor where they were parked the week before their adventure.

CHAPTER | TWENTY

A plane from the Zenith Flying Service was permitted to land at the Naval Air Base early that Saturday afternoon. After thanking the base commander, the pilots of the helicopters, crewmen, physicians, and hospital personnel, both climbed aboard the Skyline aircraft for the trip back home.

Ruth and John huddled in the back seat with a blanket across her lap. John's arm was about her. The two pilot friends rode at the controls. It had been a week–long ordeal and now both were wan looking.

As the plane landed at Sky Harbor, a large crowd of well–wishers, newspaper and television cameramen and reporters, old friends, family members, and many curiosity seekers surrounded them. Amid the din of loud talking, cheering, interviews, and the general hubbub of excitement there were the families gathered there to meet them.

Ruth's mother was there with her son and other daughter. Her mother was crying with relief to see her Ruth again. With them was Merle Agway, Ruth's erstwhile boyfriend. The boyfriend boldly announced to the press that he intended to marry Ruth. Also gathered there was Martha; Jane; their mother, Mae Livingston; and John's two young daughters. John scooped them up in his arms as they yelled in mirth. "Daddy, oh Daddy. We missed you so!"

Martha announced to the media that she and John were definitely going to reconcile. The management at Zenith told both Ruth and John to take a few days rest and then come back to work. Their salaries would be paid for all time lost to date.

The FAA Investigating teams representing the crash probe were already moving out to Mystic Island by boat to examine the plane and engine. Many newspaper and television teams were already hiring planes to fly them down to make aerial photos of the crash scene.

In the midst of the crowd scene at Sky Harbor, Mr. Herlihy of Amalgamated appeared and shook hands all around. He congratulated John and Ruth for their perseverance under duress. Then he reminded John that his new position still awaited him and to verify his start after a few days rest period. John smiled. Because of Ruth, he had that very promising position and it would be their ticket to happiness.

Now all planned to head for their homes. Ruth would pick up her car and drive her mother and sister home, followed by Merle and her brother. John would now pick up his car and drive both of his kids home to Mrs. Livingston's home for supper. Martha and Jane would ride home with their mother.

As they parted in the airport parking lot, Ruth looked back for a fleeting moment at John, a lump in her throat. John, with his two little girls in tow, looked back longingly at Ruth at the same instant. There was a union in feeling there, that could never be broken.

John, with his two girls beside him in his car, followed Mae Livingston and her two daughters back to her house for an invited supper. Mae Livingston could not be blamed for wanting to see John and Martha resurrect their marriage. It deeply hurt her to have the marriages of both of her daughters broken up.

Many thoughts ran through the mind of John versus his love for his two adorable youngsters. Kelly was eleven and little Patty was nine. But he thought that in a few short years, these girls would want to plan their own pathways through life. He would, with his new position, increase his support payments for them.

As they sat at the table in Mae's dining room, John was glad of this opportunity to be with his two beautiful, young, but growing daughters. He could never deny his devotion to them and their future welfare. As Martha now witnessed his attention to them, she now played it to her advantage.

At the supper table she started: "John, I have heard via the press that you are about to start a new position with a large corporation and while it is a flying position with a large corporation, I am willing to go along with it. Now how soon can we start looking for a big, decent house?"

John said nothing at that moment, not wishing to break up the pleasant reunion at the table. Instead he studied Martha, trying hard to understand what it was that he first saw in her twelve years before. Or was it just one of those things?

"You must realize now, John, why I had to leave you. You almost lost your life down there. Just what would your family have done if you did? Don't you owe something to your wife and children besides mental anguish? I have been tolerant with you until now. Doesn't that Reynolds girl have any sense of responsibility than to go flying off with just any man?"

"Martha, that girl had no more to do with that crash landing than I did. It was just fate."

"She must be some kind of a slut with nothing else to do but carry on with a married man."

He stood up now, enraged. He threw his napkin down on his plate in disgust. Looking straight down at Martha now, he gave full vent to his pent–up feelings. "Don't you dare call that girl a slut. She is a fine, decent girl, unlike what you have been to me. Martha, I am sorry to have to tell you this, but I have utterly no intention of a reconciliation with you. We are divorced over a year now and that is final. We are through, done, finished."

She glared at him, then tore back at him. "You mean you do not think enough of your children to put our home together again?"

"I mean this, Martha. You had one hell of a nerve to spread that press story that you did, suggesting that Ruth and I had eloped and suggesting that you were the long–suffering wife. You have never thought of anyone in your whole life but yourself. I have thought a great deal about the welfare of my children but I have now reached a definite conclusion. Even if we did foolishly reconcile, we would still be divided. We are done, Martha, and this is final."

Martha then changed her nasty tactics somewhat. "Look, John, you can't mean to say we are through. Perhaps I was a bit hasty in divorcing you but we can remarry and start anew. I will continue to tolerate you flying, if you provide me with a grand–looking house. I want a grand house like Jane here had. Give me that, and we can find happiness."

He turned his attention to Mrs. Livingston now. "Is it all right with you if I continue to see my kids here at your home?"

"Always, John. I enjoy having them here. Please come when you can." She fully realized that a reconciliation was now impossible. Martha had overreacted with her selfish demands of him.

He moved away from the table now and kissed his two children one at a time. Then he kissed Mrs. Livingston and thanked her for her overall attention to him and his kids.

"John, wait. Let's talk this over some more," pleaded Martha.

"Its too late, Martha. Go look for another rich architect. We are through for good.

"After I start my position, I will increase my support for the kids. But I owe you nothing, Martha. We both made a property settlement as part of our divorce agreement. Beyond that I owe you nothing."

"I may have to go out and find a job," Martha pleaded.

"Good. Maybe then you might learn the value of a dollar and not dream of marrying a millionaire who will shower you with money for your madcap and petty dreams."

He walked out into the cold night air and then headed for a nearby tavern. He walked in and devoured two beers, then headed home to his boarding house that he had not been near in a week. He was now alone and had a lot of positive thinking to do. He would be gone to Texas for the next two weeks of checkout training on the Meteor Executive Jet that he would be flying soon. He would not see his kids or Ruth for the two weeks he would be gone. But there was always the telephone. It would all begin as soon as he called Mr. Herlihy.

Sunday at noon, he rose out of his bed after his first comfortable sleep in a week. He bathed leisurely, shaved, and dressed up in his best suit. He then sought a telephone in the late afternoon to make a positive call to Ruth.

"Hello, yes, she is here, John. I'll call her. How are you after your ordeal down there? Here she is."

"Ruth, Honey, I love you. Will you please marry me?"

"What? Oh, John...." Then she burst into tears.

"Hello, hello, Ruth...are you okay?"

"Yes, I'm okay but repeat your last transition." She had already heard him but wanted a repeat on that proposal.

"I want to come over there. I love you. Will you marry me?"

"I'll give you my answer when I see you."

"What about Merle, Ruth?"

"I already sent him away last night, John. I told him I was sorry but there could never be anyone but you. He is gone now."

"Let's have dinner together. I'll bring the ducks for dinner," he teased.

"If you do, I'll wrap them around your neck," she laughed.

"Look, Ruth, why don't we take your mother along with us for dinner. The three of us could have a joyous fiesta."

"Oh, John, that would be a grand idea." Her heart was pounding. "John, please hurry."

He was smiling now. He jumped into his sedan and began narrowing the distance toward his beloved Ruth as fast as he could.